The Legacy

ISBN: 1-4196-0699-9
ISBN-13: 9781419606991

The Legacy

Laura Lee King

2010

Table of Contents

Acknowledgments   vii

Abstract   ix

Introduction: The Legacy   xi

Chapter I. The Origin of Humankind   1

Chapter II. The Birth and Genealogy of Jesus   5
People of Color in the Bible   14

Chapter III. Civilization in Africa   19

Chapter IV. The Social Significance of Race and Ethnicity   39

Chapter V. Reintroduction of Blacks to Americas:
       The Black Family in Slavery (1440's-1865)   43

Chapter VI. The Black Family From (1865-Present)   61

Chapter VII. The Black Church/Religion   87

The Conclusion   117
(Author's notes)

Footnotes   133

Bibliography   141

Acknowledgments

First and foremost, I want to honor my Lord and Savior Jesus Christ, for all of His blessings, mercy, and love in my life. Thanks Lord Jesus for helping me to complete this book finally.

To Mr. Homer Lee Jackson, Sr., my beloved father- my heartfelt thanks for all of his prayers and confidence in me no matter what my endeavors in life. He has since gone to be with the Lord, but his loving memory is forever in my heart. Thanks to my mother, Ella Lee Jackson, for her support and love. To Bishop Robert Lee Jackson the pastor of Acts Full Gospel Church in Oakland, California a special thanks for all of his prayers.

Thanks to my beautiful daughter Michelle Yuvienco, for her gracious support. On a regular basis finish the book mom, how much did you do today? Complete the book hurry!

I am grateful to Nell Bonaud and my god-sister, Jeanette Stoneham, for helping to organize this book. Thanks to Barbara Hecker for her technical support and Angela Grant, for her typing. My gratitude to my brothers from the Christ Community Fellowship Church, for their proofreading: Gary Benefiel, and to Al Diaz. Thanks to Jaimee Pritchett Maurer for her editing. And thanks also to Mike Valentino for his editing genius. To my granddaughter Claudia Vargas for help with the sizing of the front cover, and her mom Ines Arenas for her help with the book. To my wonderful Black History students from the University of Alaska, who encouraged me early on in the pursuit of this book, and to Pastors Eddie Jordan and Dr. Leo Scott, for their words of encouragement and prayers during the writing process.

To my Anchorage, Alaska pastor Wilbert Mickens, Jr., for his prayers and support. I am praying that one day soon the Educational Foundation will finally be up and going to help deserving college students (remember that the Foundation is to be named in my honor)!

Abstract

This book is an Afro-centric view of the origins of man. It confronts the long-established legacy of racism, which runs rampant throughout the United States of America. It is an attempt to help people, of all ethnicities/races, to view history differently. It challenges us to ask some tough questions. Has history been written "by the victors?" Do standard textbooks really strive to teach accurate renditions of world history? Has politics, driven by racial prejudice, distorted genuine scholarship? Through this study, we will examine these and many other important issues. We must all become "change agents" when it comes to interpreting history, if our intent is to interpret it fairly.

We must be willing to listen to different perspectives if we want to be truly informed. Moreover, it is vital that we familiarize ourselves with beliefs that challenge Westernized traditions that have been accepted and passed on us truth for centuries. In short, we must find the truth for ourselves.

Some of the works that are referenced within the pages of this book will, undoubtedly, be criticized as highly controversial. Yet, controversial does not mean inaccurate, and often works that are on the cutting edge of scholarship are initially rejected – until they are later proven to be right. Most importantly, though, it is my hope that readers will obtain knowledge of God's wisdom, which is depicted throughout the Holy Bible—God loves all His children whether they are white, yellow, red, brown, or black.

(Some words will be used interchangeably: Caucasian (White); and Black (African Americans). The term "Negro" will not be used, unless it is quoted. "Negro" is Spanish for "black;" but has held many negative connotations for Blacks throughout American history.

*{And ye shall know the truth and the truth shall make you free
-John 8:32}*

Preface

The Legacy

"You know, when black ice is on the roadway, it is very diffi-cult to see regardless of the amount of daylight- racism is like that. For instance on Sunday, in every state in America, there will be White churches having their services and Black churches having theirs; both serving the same God," said my brother, Pastor Robert "Bob" Jackson of Acts Full Gospel Church in Oakland, California.

Some Black Christians who have visited Caucasian churches have felt left out of White worship services, and vice versa. Most Blacks pre-fer the energy of Black services, although some Blacks have joined White churches over the years, integrating more church services.

The church people attend is a matter of preference and should not become a racial issue; people will go where they feel the most comfortable. Neither the names of the church nor its members are as important as the Word of God being taught and people growing with the Lord. As long as we continue to reach out to one another other, across barriers, and respect each other's perspective- there is hope.

The first purpose of this book is to provide a biblical framework for the origins of humankind. According to the Bible, God created man in His own image and likeness. Where mankind has failed is by mak-ing God in *their* image. Mankind has tended to describe God in their likeness, mainly Caucasian, in recent years some Afro-centric images have appeared in some Churches. In man's attempt to make God in his own image, truth becomes evasive and often falsified. It is an egocentric quest, where human beings take center stage and basically pay lip service to the God who created them.

The second purpose of this book is to provide factual information involving the many contributions made to the World and to America by the people now known as Blacks or African Americans.

Driven by pride, in Biblical times and throughout history, groups have come to hate each other for various reasons. It began as early as biblical days within the original family, when Cain, in a fit of jealousy murdered his brother Abel. Clearly, this hatred had nothing to do with race/color. Indeed, even in the rivalry and warfare amongst ancient nations, this loathing had little to do with the color of one's skin. Most people in Biblical times lived in the desert, arid areas, and they were very similar in appearance and complexion. Since mankind came from one source, it never really made sense to discriminate or to treat groups differently based on skin tone. Such bigotry was virtually unheard of (as far as we can know) in antiquity.

The world began with one man and one woman. All humans can be traced back to Adam and Eve in the Holy Bible, in the first book of Genesis. Whether people choose to believe it or not, all humans are related. Scientific findings have concluded all humans are related despite their ethnical origins. Humans share the same biological components that distinguish *Homo sapiens* from other species of animals; all humans are 98% the same.

Why then, some may ask, do we have so much conflict and strife? Because of sin in the world, there has always been war, but not over the color of one's skin. Tribal wars would erupt based on disputes for territory, resources, or similar reasons. The victor would take over the defeated tribe and their possessions. This led to slavery, which most biblical societies practiced. However, the slavery of ancient times was very different from the slavery America engaged in. Race had nothing to do with it whatsoever – the exact opposite of American history, where race was the pivotal factor that laid the foundation of the institution of slavery.

One of the vestiges of slavery, historically, has been the manner in which Black people have had to interact with White people. In the not so distant past, Blacks were taught to be careful of their responses and demeanor in the presence of Whites. Like road signs that caution of unsuspected dangers, for example the "black ice" scenario, experience had taught most African Americans to be wary when dealing with Caucasians. Hence, came the shuffling of feet, looking down, and never looking directly into a White person's face; if one did, it was taken as a sign of aggression or hostility which could lead to retribution. For Blacks this form of docility was necessary in order not to be hurt, because if the White man was angry, it was lawful for them to treat Blacks with brutality. Though Blacks were technically free after the Civil War, they still were not treated – not even close – as being equal citizens within their own country. A double standard of behavior was firmly in place, often codified by law, and at the very least in the cultural mindset of just about all people, on both sides of the racial divide.

By educating themselves in the ways of White people, Blacks managed to avoid many pitfalls; it was a type of survival course young Black men had to go through if they wanted to live. They were indoctrinated to the ways and methods of the White group. This knowledge was passed down from family to family, from generation to generation. This insured that the ingrained prejudice of Whites would continue unabated. And how could it not? Nobody was ever taught differently, which is precisely the problem with prejudice. It operates out of sheer ignorance; people fear what's not like them. Prejudice is a learned behavior for all ethnicities, not just Blacks and Whites.

Racism is hard to recognize in America because it comes with many masks. Racism is often excused as "tradition" or "the American way." That's because it is a "sensitive" issue that people would prefer to just wish away. But that is no solution at all. The real issues with racism are denial and ignorance. We have passed legislation to make changes in the American culture to promote equality. Many people may believe, with these new laws in place, that there are no racial issues left in America. However the problem remains.

The truth is, however, all the legislation in the world can't reach people's hearts. People will not change their entrenched views until they learn that what they are doing is wrong, and change is the only answer. But hardened hearts, by their very nature, resist change. Therefore, racism has become covert; it is difficult to discern, very much like black ice on the roadways in winter. In America, racism is a problem for most minority groups, and lower economic classes. As long as Americans continue to teach their children to be prejudiced against certain people, those who are different from their own group, racism will continue to grow and plague America. It infects everything it touches, be it individuals, family members, the business world, the arts, politics, religion…its ugly tentacles have a sickeningly long reach.

Children study what is said and done, mannerisms and slang, and learn from their parents. The question is does this kind of racism have to continue in perpetuity? Or is there a way for us to break the chain of ignorance that forges new links with every coming generation? There is hope. But it will take a different kind of law and a change of mankind's heart to eradicate this problem. Nothing outside us can effect such change; it has to come from within. With God's help this change will come about; Americans truly united can make all the difference this country needs. With this challenge comes tremendous opportunity: America may yet live up to her stated ideals of freedom, equality and justice for all.

God awaits America's personal commitment to alleviate racial problems through faithful adherence to His just laws. As Christians, we can do it! Americans must do it! Americans need to set the example for the rest of the world. And there is no better place to start than by confronting the realities of history in this great nation. By researching and finding the true history as it relates to Africans in a fair, logical and unbiased manner.

{Let us make man in our own image, according to our likeness}
-Genesis 1:26

Chapter I.

Looking Back:
Origin of Humankind

Ultra Violet rays activate melanin, which is a chemical in human skin. Where one lives geographically and how much sun a person is exposed to determines an individual's skin color. The more intense the Ultra Violet radiation, the darker the skin will become. Jesus was probably olive skinned because of where he lived.

According to Genesis 2:7:

{And the Lord God formed man of the dust of the ground, and breathed into his nostrils the breath of life; and man became a living soul.] [1]

God used the dust of the earth to form man. The Master Planner formed man in His own image. To go a bit further with this idea, it was probably *not* white dust.

{When God created man in His image, He gave him dominion over the earth and all its creatures. God blessed humans and decreed they *be fruitful and multiply*. Indeed, there soon was history's first "baby boom." Genesis 2:10-15 identifies four key rivers where the burgeoning human population thrived. }[2]

There are the Pishon and Gihon rivers, associated with the ancient Hebrew land, Cush (present day Ethiopia); as well as the Hiddekel (Tigris) and the Euphrates rivers located in southeastern Turkey, which flow into present day Syria and Iraq. These rivers were the birthplace of humankind. It is easy to assume, given the arid climate of the region, which the first humans were likely dark skinned.

It is important to establish that there was but one race of people. We all share the same beginnings and evidence exists that point toward humankind evolving from a single family. God created the first man with His own hands (Genesis 2:7) and *all* of humankind has developed according to God's plan. If God had wanted people to look alike, He could have very well performed this task. Without a doubt, diversity has been a key element of the divine plan from the very beginning.

A person's individual prejudices are often rooted in the idea that one race is superior to another, and some use Biblical history to justify their biases. It seems clear, however, that such people have twisted their presentation of scriptural facts in an attempt to prop up their own faulty thinking. *And the whole earth was of one language, and of one speech*

{(Genesis 11:1) suggests that God never created any one group to be superior over any other group.} [3]

Later, when Moses describes the Table of Nations, which lists their lineage, he takes the time to write about a descendant of Cush named Nimrod. He was the first king, the very beginning of the monarchy system. Nimrod was a mighty hunter "blessed by God." He reigned over large areas of land, which included Babel, Erech, Accad, and Calneh in the land of Sinar. Through military campaigns, he extended his empire to Assyria. He built Rehoboth-Ir, Calah, and Resen, with the main city of Nineveh as the capital of his empire. The population grew and spread eastward. Fertile land was discovered in the plains of Babylon and it became heavily populated. The people along with their leader Nimrod who lived there began to talk about building a great city with a temple tower that would reach to the heavens. This was to be a proud, eternal monument to themselves and their own ingenuity, independent of God. They reasoned that this tower would prevent them from being scattered all over the land. This tower would stand tall so they could walk into God's holy abode.

> {Genesis 11:6-9: And the Lord said, Behold, the people is one, and they have all one language; and this they begin to do: and now nothing will be restrained from them, which they have imagined to do. And God said, let us go down, and there confound their language, that they may not understand one another's speech. *So the Lord scattered them abroad from hence upon the face of all the earth; and they left off to build the city.*
> *Therefore is the name of it called Babel; because the Lord did there confound the language of all the earth; and from thence did the Lord scatter them abroad upon the face of all the earth.}* [4]

This scattering explains why today, we have a variety of cultures, languages, and people of different colors all over the world. The original unity no longer exists. Human beings are now widely dispersed throughout the globe. Yet this story from the Bible tells us why this happened – and it has nothing to do with superiority. It was, instead, God's way of teaching an important lesson to mankind: that all of us rely on God's grace for all that we have, and that, separated from God, people will separate themselves from each other as well, leading to ignorance, violence and hatred.

It is important to note that Jesus spoke Aramaic. This was the common language of the early first century Palestinians. When exploring the meaning of words it is good to use the actual language or derivative of it in its initial form. For example, Hebrew translated into Hebrew, and Latin into Latin. If Jesus' words had been translated into Aramaic it would tend to offer a meaning much closer to the actual meaning!

{Behold, a virgin shall be with child, and shall bring forth a son, and they shall call his name Emmanuel, which being interpreted is, God with us.}
-Matthew 1:23

Chapter II.
The Birth and Genealogy of Jesus Christ

It is hopefully understood that Jesus was with His father God from the beginning. As Jesus is Alpha and Omega the beginning and the end! Jesus was in the Garden of Eden with His father when God said: *Let us make man in our image, after our likeness….* The person God was speaking to was the Lord Jesus Christ. Jesus decided to leave heaven to come to earth as a God/man to die for the sins of the world. It was the only way that mankind could be saved. We are looking at Jesus' birth; His immaculate birth and His genealogy.

Matthew 1-16 describes the lineage of Jesus Christ, the Savior to all regardless of ethnicity:

{The book of generation of Jesus Christ, the son of David, the son of Abraham;

Abraham begat Isaac; and Isaac begat Jacob; and Jacob begat Judas and his brethren;

and Judas begat Phares and Zara of Thamar; and Pheres begat Esrom; and Estrom begat Aram;

and Aram Begat Amindab; and Amindab begat Naasson; and Naasson begat Salmon; and Salmon begat Boaz and Rachab; and Boaz begat Obed of Ruth; and Obed begat Jesse;

and Jesse begat David the King; and David the King begat Solomon of her that had been the wife of Urias (Bethsheba);

and Solomon begat Robosam; and Robosam begat Abia; and Abia begat Asa;

and Asa begat Josaphat; and Josaphat begat Joran; and Joran begat Ozias;

and Ozias begat Joatham; and Joatham begat Achaz; and Achaz begat Ezekias;

and Ezekias begat Manasses; and Manasses begat Amon; and Amon begat Josias; and Josias begat Jechonias and his brethren, about the time they were carried away to Babylon;

and after they were brought to Babylon, Jechonias begat Salathiel; and Salathiel begat Zorobabel;
and Zorobabel begat Abuid; and Abuid begat Eliakim; and Eliakim begat Azor;

and Azor begat Sadoc; and Sadoc begat Achim; and Achim begat Eluid;

and Eluid begat Eleazor; and Eleazor begat Matthan; and Matthan begat Jacob;

and Jacob begat Joseph, the husband of Mary of whom was born Jesus, who is called Christ.} [1]

The birth of Jesus was the source of much speculation, surprise, and controversy among first century Hebrews and the debate continues to the present day.

{The birth of Jesus Christ was prophesied in Isaiah 53:1-12. The Bible describes how it was possible for Mary to have a baby without being touched by a man. } [2]

{Now the birth of Jesus Christ was on this wise: When as his mother, Mary was espoused to Joseph, before they came together, she was found with child of the Holy Ghost Matthew 1:18 } [3]

Behold, a virgin shall be with child, and shall bring forth a son and they shall call his name Emmanuel, which means, "God with us." Joseph knew her not till she had brought forth her firstborn son; and called his name Jesus. Matthew 2:1-3, 4

{Now when Jesus was born in Bethlehem of Judea in the days of Herod the King, behold, there came wise men from the east to Jerusalem. Saying where is he that is born King of the Jews? For we have seen his star in the East, and are come to worship him. When Herod the king had heard these things, he was troubled, and all Jerusalem with him.} [4]

The three wise men praised and worshipped the child, and gave him gifts. After they departed, an angel appeared to Joseph in a dream and told him to flee with his family into Egypt. The evil King Herod wanted the baby killed.

After the death of Herod, an angel again appeared and told Joseph to return with his family to Israel.
The Jewish historian and military leader in Galilee Flavius Josephus, who lived in the first century, said:

{That Jesus was a man of plain looks, extremely learned, and full of vigor, with dark skin} [5]

It would seem that Jesus took on the looks of an everyday Palestinian. He did not want to be treated differently.
Daniel wrote in 7:9:

{I beheld till the thrones were cast down, and the Ancient of days did sit, whose garment was white as snow, and the hair on his head like the pure wool; his throne was like the fiery flame, and his wheels as burning fire.} [6]

The prophecy, revealed to Daniel, concerned the judgment of the Gentiles and establishment of an everlasting Kingdom of God.

{However, the King James translators did not forget to use the word "Greece" in reference to Daniel's prophecy. The same translators saw "Sudanese" Africans in chains boarding slave ships, yet they called them Negroes! But when these Sudanese Kings sat on the thrones of Egypt, the translators called them Ethiopians.}[7]

John, in Revelation 1:14-15 sees similar physical features in the Messianic figure now called the Son of Man whose features are much like those previously noted in Daniel 7:9

{His head and his hairs were white like wool, as white as snow; and his eyes were as a flame of fire; His feel like unto fine brass, as if they burned in a furnace; and his voice as the sound of many waters. }[8]

This author believes:

That the biblical description tends to describe people of color when correctly translated, there is no mention those of Caucasian descent directly. Yet, people of color were/are in the Bible; it was hidden for centuries and their place in history denied.

The most important point of all of this, of course, is the identity of Jesus. Christians see Him as God incarnate, and the Savior of the world. Naturally, then, it is not surprising that different groups of people would want to claim Him as one of their own. The same can be said of other important biblical figures. Indeed, there exists a vast amount of confusion that seemingly stems from the deliberate European attempt to conceal the ethnic identity of some of the people of the Bible. When missionaries first went into Africa, they brought the Bible and the gun. When they left, they had gold and diamonds, and Africans had the Bible. But many of these missionaries were not spreading the true Gospel at all. They had a twisted, completely non-Christian concept of African people. Some of the worst of them actually believed that Africans were without souls and were heathens. Did they believe

that God only cared for Whites? This reflected an extremely racist ideology on the part of European Christians, a worldview that prevailed
for numerous centuries.

The Introduction to the Original African Heritage Study Bible
states:

> {The origin of this people has been shrouded in the mysteries of
> the various versions and translations of the Bible (especially The
> King James) for many years this was due, in part, to the misinter-
> pretations of those who rendered the original translations from
> Hebrew and Greek into Latin, English, and other languages. How-
> ever, a large portion of the confusion stems from the deliberate
> Euro centric attempts to conceal what today would be called the
> racial and/or ethnic identity of the people of the Bible.} [9]

The Introduction continues:

> {In the name of religion, grave injustices have been perpetu-
> ated upon the entire world. These injustices have caused insur-
> mountable suffering and pain. It is the collective consensus of
> the translators and their interpretations of this version of the
> Bible that this cycle of darkness must be broken, for the truth is
> the light, and with the truth all captives shall be set free.} [10]

The Introduction concludes that:

> {The Bible is multicultural and multiracial with its purpose of be-
> ing a universalism of the salvation story. Europeans are in the
> Bible. So are Asians and others. For example, in the New Testa-
> ment the Apostle Paul clearly intends to travel to Spain (Romans
> 15:24, 28) significantly, included are also Blacks and descriptions
> of Africa. } [11]

The concept of inclusion is very important as the Bible is very
inclusive, and people from other lands are written about and people
from various backgrounds were also written about and given credence
for being able to be "adopted" into the family of God, for example

the Ethiopian Eunuch of great authority under Candace queen of the Ethiopians, who had the charge of all her treasure, and had come to Jerusalem for the worship. (Acts 8:26-39) (This author's paraphrased). Phillip listened to what the angel of the Lord said to him, saying arise, and go toward the south unto the way that goeth down from Jerusalem unto Gaza. Phillip saw an Ethiopian reading Isaiah from pages of the Bible. And asked him if he understood what he was reading, and he said he needed someone to help him to understand. Phillip told him the meanings of the scriptures and he wanted to be baptized, Phillip baptized him. The Spirit of the Lord caught away Phillip. And the Eunuch went away rejoicing!

{Another example (John 4:1-30) is when Jesus spoke to a Samaritan woman at the well; this was not done as Samaritans were considered to be inferior to the Jews. Actually this unnamed woman was the very first evangelist as she ran and told the men what Jesus had told her.} [12]

From the Original African Heritage Study Bible:

{England was very familiar with the black man of Africa during the seventeenth century. The Muslims had long since given Africa the name "El Bilad es Sudan," translated "Land of the Blacks," or the Blackman's Land." England knew well that during the early days of the Old Testament, Africa was called "The Land of Ham." England had entered the slave trade as early as 1552; Queen Elizabeth had money invested in the slave trade and in the colonies of the Americas to where they were going. When the King James translators completed the translation in 1611, the black presence had been a part of the English colony scenario. But the translators called them Negroes instead of Ethiopians, hoping that the common minds of that day would see only color. } [13]

One would have to believe had the Africans been called by their proper title Ethiopians it might have made a difference in how the slave trade was conducted. On the other hand perhaps the money to be made from the trade of human cargo blinded most people of that day.

All people are descended from Noah after the flood no matter how they looked outwardly.

> {The Egyptians appear to have been looked upon as black Africans by the other people of the then known world. In the fifth century, B.C. the Greek historian Herodotus referred to the Egyptians as being "black skinned with woolly hair." Note: That in chapter 10 of Genesis all the races of the world are described as having been derived from Adam and Eve.} [14]

Some European countries did acknowledge the fact that the Africans were a great people:

> {Black Africans also appear in the history of Greece and Rome.
> The Greeks in particular seem to have had a high regard for them. In the Iliad, Homer speaks of the gods feasting with the "blameless Ethiopians." In the first Century B.C., the Greek historian Siculus attributed the fact the Ethiopians (a term used by the Greeks for black Africans). Have the oldest civilization due to their closeness to the ripening warmth if the sun.
> It should be noted also that at this time the Greeks tended to think of the fairer-skinned Nordic peoples as being an inferior race of barbarians} [15]

Greek history has recorded that the fairer-skinned Nordic people were an inferior race of barbarians early in history. Where exactly is this type of information readily available in American History books?

According to James W. Peebles: One of the ten contributors to the Original African Heritage Study Bible:

> {Probably the greatest act that crystallized the justification of European slave trading was the Catholic priest Bartholomo de las Casas' writing in his encyclical to the papacy that these people (the Africans were without souls and suitable for the torturous work in the Americas. } [16]

De la Casas was not the only leader that felt as he did, Africans were seen as heathens without souls. However, the King James translators did not forget to uses the word "Greece" in reference to Daniel's prophecy. The same translators saw "Sudanese" Africans in chains boarding slave ships, yet they called them Negroes! Yet when these Sudanese Kings sat on the thrones of Egypt, the translators called them Ethiopians. How can the word <u>Negro</u> come out of the word Ethiopian? Without a single missed step a King was relegated to the status of peon.

God's prophesy upon Israel to "bring thee into Egypt again with ships" was fulfilled:

{Over 100 million people were either taken captives or killed in the slave wars. About one-third of the Africans taken from their homes died on the way to the coast and at the embarkation stations, and another third dies at sea, so that only one third finally survived to become the laborers in the New World. } [17]

Millions of Africans were taken from Africa:

{And the Lord shall bring thee into Egypt again with ships, by the way whereof I spake unto thee, Thou shalt see it no more again: and there ye shall be sold unto your enemies for bondmen and bondwomen, and no man shall buy you. Deuteronomy 28:68 } [18]

In other words no man could keep them from being sent into slavery. Once taken into slavery men auctioned the slaves off the highest bidder: One of the largest auction blocks was located in Washington, D.C. near to where the White House is located. There is a plethora of materials out that prove the heritage of Jesus.

In recent years in America, there has been a proliferation of books and pamphlets, which represent a resurgence of what may be called an Afro-centric approach to the Bible. During the biblical era in history, race was of no importance; racial prejudice or racial topologies did not exist. However, in modern American society, anyone with a minuscule amount of African ancestry is considered Black. Accordingly, this would include Jesus and His mother, Mary, who had numerous people of color within their bloodline.

St. Paul declared in Galatians 3:28:

{There is neither Jew nor Greek, there is neither bond nor free, there is neither male nor female; for ye are all one in Christ Jesus.} [19]

Paul could have added there is neither black, white, brown, yellow, nor red. The mere fact that he did not mention <u>color</u> is an indication <u>color</u> had no importance at this time in Biblical history.

People of Color in the Bible

The Original African Heritage Study Bible

This section is to prove that there were many persons of color in the Holy Bible. The translations did not always tend to describe them as such. But thanks to the Original African Heritage Bible the persons will identified and it will become clear.

The Queen of Sheba

The Queen of Sheba was from the Sheba province, an area at the southern tip of the Arabian Peninsula. Born to the family line of Shem and Ham, she was a descendant of Abraham and Keturah. The Queen of Sheba was also Queen of Ethiopia. Praised for her beauty and wealth, she earned international acclaim.

> {I Kings 10:1 tell of her visit to King Solomon where she marveled at the wisdom of his response to her many questions. King Solomon and the Queen of Sheba exchanged many gifts of great value and importance; she even bore him a son, Menelik I.} [20]

Zipporah

She is identified as Moses' Cushite wife. It is said that Moses' brother, Aaron and his sister, Miriam did not like her. Some said it was because of the religion that Zipporah believed in while, according to the Original African Heritage Study Bible, others claimed it was because Zipporah, Jethro's daughter, was a Black woman. According to the Original African Heritage Study Bible, Moses was an African Hebrew.

Numbers 12:1 states:
{And Miriam and Aaron spoke against Moses because of the Ethiopian women who he had married, for he had married an Ethiopian woman and she was of a different religion.} [21]

The Bible does not state that her ethnicity or color was associated with the displeasure Aaron and Miriam expressed.

{The Lord God heard these murmurings, and the clouds engulfed Miriam [22]

When the clouds dissipated Miriam was "white" as snow, a form of leprosy. Aaron went to Moses, and asked his father to save Miriam from this horrible disease. Moses implored the Lord God for mercy, and was told Miriam would have to suffer for seven days in isolation before reappearing in a healed state. This curse came from God, not man.

Ebedmelech

{This Ethiopian eunuch saved the life of the prophet Jeremiah. He saw the miserable fate of Jeremiah, who had been thrown into the dungeon where he sunk into the mire. Jeremiah: 38:6 } [23]

{Concerned Jeremiah would die in these conditions, Ebedmelech reported to King Zedekiah, asking if they might not remove Jeremiah from this desperate situation. The King allowed this rescue, and sent Ebedmelech to rescue Jeremiah from the dungeon. Still in prison but in more satisfactory conditions, Jeremiah was then able to plead his case to the King, and was eventually freed. Jeremiah 38:1-28. } [24]

Hagar

{Hagar was the Egyptian handmaiden of Abraham's wife, Sarah, who was barren. Sarah offered Hagar to satisfy Abraham, who desired a son. Hagar bore Abraham a son, Ishmael; making the Arabs first cousins to the Israelites. Genesis 16:1.} [25]

Tirhakah

A king of Ethiopia and Egypt in the twenty-fifth dynasty, Tirhakah was the opponent to the Assyrian king for the domination of Palestine. He attempted to defend Egypt against the Assyrian kings, but was defeated in the delta and driven south into Upper Egypt, where he maintained a rule of some dignity at Thebes. 2 Kings 19:9-13. [26]

Also in Isaiah 37:9-10:

{And he heard say concerning Tirhakah, King of Ethiopia, he is come forth to make war with thee, and when he heard it, he sent messengers to Hezekiah, saying, Thus shall ye speak to Hezekiah, King of Juda, saying let not they God, in whom you trusted deceive thee, saying, Jerusalem shall not be delivered into the hand of the king of Assyria}. [27]

Asenath

Asenath was the Egyptian wife of Joseph, son of Jacob (renamed Israel), given to him by the Pharaoh. Asenath and Joseph had two sons, Manasseh and Ephraim.
Genesis 41:45 states:

{And Pharaoh called Joseph's name Zaph'-nath-pa-a-a-new; and he gave him a wife, As'e-nath, the daughter of Pot-I-ph'-rah, priest of On. And Joseph went out over all the land of Egypt}. [28]

Simon of Cyrene

Simon was ordered to help Jesus to carry the cross, and Cyrene was an ancient city in Libya, Africa.

St. Mark 15:21, 32.
{And they compelled one Simon, a Cy-re'-ni-an, who passed by, coming out of the country, the father of Alexander and Rufus, to help Jesus to bear his cross. } [29]

Controversy raged over the color of numerous others, among them, King Solomon. Reading the Songs of Solomon, the king's lyrical prose, some conclude he too was a Black man. Solomon's song-like book was devoted to his relationship with Makeda, better known as the Queen of Sheba.

There are many passages that speak to the people of color in the Bible, especially when areas such as Egypt and Ethiopia are mentioned. In the Bible, Egypt is mentioned 100 times and Ethiopia is mentioned 40 times. If these people and places were not important, then God would not have included them in His holy book. Moses was a man of color; if he had not been, then the following from
Exodus could not have taken place:

{And the Lord said furthermore said unto him; put now thine hand into thy bosom. And he put his hand into his bosom: and when he took it out, behold, his hand was leprous as snow…. And he said, put thine hand into thy bosom again. And he put his hand into his bosom again; and plucked it out of his bosom, and, behold, it was turned again as his other flesh. Exodus 4: 6-7}. [30]

Moses, descendant of Abraham, was born in Egypt, a Hebrew. While engaging in dialogue with God, Moses was shown an outstanding sign of God's power by placing his hand on his bosom it became "leprous as snow." The predominant and characteristic form of leprosy in the Old Testament was of a *white* variety, covering the entire body or a large part of its surface. This act of turning "tanned" flesh white and then back again was truly a miracle.

If people's skin had originally been white in color, the color would have remained the same or somewhat similar, however it came as amazement to Moses upon seeing the difference in his skin tone. Leprosy was a sickness and it was deadly in many cases. It is this author's contention that a mild case would render the people light, pale, or "whitish" similar to being an albino without color. These people would group together and move away from the pigmented others. Which would lead into another group of people with a fair complexion, it also depended on the location that they lived whether they remained "light."

{And I had made of one blood all nations of men for to dwell on all the face of the earth, and hath determined the times before appointed, and the bounds of their habitation.
-Acts 17:26}

Chapter III.
Civilization in Africa

It seems civilization started in the great river valleys of Africa and the Middle East; the Fertile Crescent in the Near East and along the narrow ribbon of the Nile in Africa. Interestingly enough the Greeks did not have any trouble recording information concerning Africans. The Greeks and their written documents have shed much light on this "dark continent." However, the traditional European historians neglected to research the Greek findings. The many "firsts" and significant contributions made to the world by Africans would still be "lost" had it not been for the marvelous Greeks and their honesty.

{According to Lerone Bennett, Jr. in his book <u>Before the Mayflower</u> stated:

When the human drama opened, Africans were on the scene and acting. For a long time, in fact, the only people on the scene were Africans. For some 600,000 years, Africa and Africans led the world. Were these people who gave the world fire and tools, and cultivated grain-were they Negroes? } [1]

Sometime the color issue had some type of blinding effect upon the accepting of the truth if it did not fit within a certain criteria. The problem here is that most people have never heard of these "gifts" made to the entire world by the members of this proud "dark continent."

{Bennett continues:

Civilization started in the great river valleys of Africa and Asia, in the Fertile Crescent in the Near East, and along the narrow ribbon of the Nile in Africa. In the Nile Valley, that beginning was an African as well as an Asian achievement Blacks or the people who would be considered Blacks today, were among the first people to use tools, paint pictures, plant seeds and worship gods. Back there, in the beginning, blackness was not an occasion for obloquy. In fact, the reverse seems to have been true. White men were sometimes ridiculed for the "unnatural whiteness of their skin."} [2]

Lerone Bennett, Jr. often stated that slavery was not new, it was as old as the Bible. It seems that most of the people in ancient times were of color. The people of color were honored and known throughout the ancient world.

{According to Bennett:
Slavery, in one form or another, has been practiced in every country known to man. Slavery was old when Moses was young. In Plato's Athens and Caesar's Rome, men-white, black, and brown -were bought and sold. Slavery existed in the Middle Ages in Christian Europe and in "pagan" Africa. } [3]

Bennett stated that men from all backgrounds have been enslaved at some point over history. Color has intentionally been the primary focus for abuse from Europeans towards Africans. Early traders and foreigners did not seem to mind trading with Africans. The distinction between one skin color and another was not significant during this period in history. The skin tone of a person did not indicate one's race or ethnic origin, however, the clothing one wore spoke to the status one held and seemed of primary importance. Europeans used religion to justify their exploitation of people of color, including Africans and Native Americans. Europeans felt it necessary to "save the heathens" by introducing them to Christianity.

Africans led the way for trading in the known world, and they were treated as equals prior to the time of Columbus. Africans were leaders at that period in history. Greeks wrote their history and included Africans in their recordings. Bennett includes some of the better-known classical Greek writers.

{Bennett stated:
Homer, Herodotus, Pliny, Diodorus, and other classical writers repeatedly praised the Ethiopians. "The annals of the great early nations of Asia Minor are full of them," Lady Flora Louisa Lugard writes. "The mosaic records allude to them frequently; but while they are described as the most powerful, the most just, and the most beautiful of the human race, they are constantly spoken of as black, and there seems to be no other conclusion to be drawn, than that at that remote period of history the leading race of the Western World was a black race. } [4]

What a wonderful description of a group of Africans and to be considered so is a very honorable testimony of any people. The leading race of the Western World was a black race.

{Franz Boas as stated in Bennett's Before the Mayflower:
"It seems likely that at a time when the European was still satisfied with rude stone tools, the African had invented and adopted the art of smelting iron. Consider for a moment what this had meant for the advance of the human race....A great progress was made when copper found in large nuggets was hammered out into tools and later on shaped by smelting, and when bronze was introduced many items were made; however, but the true advancement of industrial life did not begin until the hard iron was discovered. It seems not unlikely that the people who made the marvelous discovery of reducing iron ore smelting were the African Negroes. Neither ancient Europe nor western Asia nor ancient China knew iron, and everything points to its introduction from Africa. } [5]

At the time of the great African discoveries toward the end of the past century, the trade of blacksmithing was found all over Africa, from north to south, and from east to west. With their simple bellows and a charcoal fire, they reduced the ore that was found in many parts of the continent and forged implements of great usefulness and beauty; the world has Africa to thank for the many inventions and advancements that helped all of mankind!

Iron smelting and other items needed for mankind to survive were discoveries made in Africa; for it seems that the only people doing anything at that time in history were Africans. Again it seems until recent times that most of this factual information had been omitted from the history books. Very few African contributions have been recorded. However, the Greeks, along with Dr. L.S. B. Leakey's discoveries, led the way to uncovering the truth about Africa, and its people. To this day Leakey's findings have not been disproved and he is a member of the European "so-called" racial group. Leakey informed the world about the truth at a time that doing so could have ostracized him. God made sure that the truth was recorded.

{According to J. A. Rogers's:
In his "Light in Africa," a portion of the globe to which the stalwart Anglo-Saxon Stanley gave the name of 'dark' and 'darkest,' relating to the African Continent. Light upon the people of that continent whose children we are accustomed to regard as types of natural servility with no recorded history." But "The spell has been broken. The buried treasure of antiquity again revisits the sun." He gave abundant proof of rich archaeological and other finds, which since have been supplemented by the Mond Expedition in Sudan; the researches of Professor L.S. B. Leakey in East Africa; and Professors Broom and Dart in South Africa. Leakey discovered remains of the Boskop Man, a bushman type of some 30,000 years ago; and Broom and Dart types that go still farther back. Their researches appear to bear out what and earlier anthropologist, Prichard, said in his "Physical History of Man." Namely the primitive stocks of men were probably Negroes and I know of no argument to be set on the other side." Europe was itself still joined to Africa it was tropical and was inhabited by Negroes} [6]

There are abundant artifacts and documented materials to warrant acceptance of Africa as the birthplace for all of humanity.

{According to Gerald Horne:
The human race probably developed in Asia or Africa. Modern people were present in Europe 50,000 years ago, and they may have been there 5,000 years before that. It is now believed that the first human beings reached America possibly more than 15,000 years ago. There is a general agreement that they came via the Bering Strait.} [7]

According to many historians, archaeologists, and researchers, such as Leakey, Rogers's, Van Sertima, Wiener, and Bennett, whom studied Africans and their contributions, all agree that Africa was and is the "Cradle of Civilization." Civilization started in the great river valley of Africa and Asia, in the Fertile Crescent in the Near East along the narrow ribbon of the Nile in Africa. These African people were the first people to use tools, paint pictures, and plant seeds.

{According to Berkin, et al:
Some 1,000,000 years ago, humans began to spread out from the grasslands of Africa, traveling by way of Asia, on through Siberia these people reached the land bridge and crossed over populating the Western Hemisphere some time later. The people came, anthropologists believe between 12,000 and 30,000 years ago during the last Ice Age, a time when much of the earth's water was frozen in huge glaciers, the crossing is called the land bridge where the Bering Strait now flows, (it is speculated that the land bridge, fell away and is now under the Bering Strait). Theorists think that the hunter-gatherers were following the giant mammoths and mastodons, trying to keep up with their food supply.} [8]

A number of scientists, scholars both in ancient and modern times, have concluded that the world's first civilization was the creation of a people known as Ethiopians. Much of the recent information that has been "unearthed" came about because of the willingness of Greeks. They wrote about the African contribution to civilization. The Greeks also wrote about how they borrowed scientific, legal, medical, and mathematical information from Africans. For instance, the world owes the very name Ethiopia to the ancient Greeks, for when these

Hellenes first came in contact with the dark inhabitants of Africa; they called the Africans "burnt faces."

Most World History books attribute all of the above-mentioned contributions to Greeks. It is well recorded and heralded that Greece led the way to modern civilization, although they borrowed their contributions from their associates and traders in Africa. Nevertheless, if Africans were mentioned, evidently African discoveries were left out of the books. Bennett stated that many European traders found Africans to be equals and partners in trade and commerce, where both Europeans and Africans benefited.

{Bennett continues:
The Ethiopians claimed to be the spiritual fathers of Egyptian civilization. Diodorus Siculus, the Greek historian who wrote in the first century B.C., said: "The Ethiopians conceived themselves to be of greater antiquity than any other nation; and it is probable that, born under the sun's path, its warmth may have ripened them earlier than other men. They supposed themselves to be the inventors of worship, of festivals, of solemn assemblies, of sacrifices, and every religious practice."} [9]

Ethiopia is a very ancient nation; they were no doubt among the earlier humans to make discoveries that others have relied on throughout history, especially religion.

Author's note: {It is also important to note that the word slave is a European term and comes from the Slavic language}. Europe had its share of slavery; it was not written about in literature for the most part.

Historically speaking, Europeans were sold into slavery earlier in history. People who themselves were humiliated and downtrodden would do such cruel and inhumane things to other people. It seems to this author that Africans were the victims of a maniacal scheming, contemptuous group of angry people getting their revenge for the mistreatment that they had endured for a period of time. Most of this information was not written about, it fact it seems some people went to great lengths to hid these facts. Interestingly, Europeans see Egypt as being separate from Africa, when in fact Egypt is in North Africa not the Middle East.

> {Bennett further stated:
> How did the Egyptians see themselves? They painted themselves in three colors: black, reddish-brown, yellow. The color white was available to them, but they used it to portray blue-eyed, white-skinned foreigners. One of the great murals of Egyptian art is the procession from a tomb of Thebes in the time of Thotmes III. The Egyptians and Ethiopians in the procession are painted in the usual brown and black colors. Thirty-seven whites in the procession are rendered in white tones. Who were they? G.A. Hoskins said they were probably "white slaves of the king of Ethiopia sent to the Egyptian king as the most acceptable present." } [10]

Amazingly enough Egyptians did not regard themselves as being "White." Far from it they seemed content to portray themselves with darker hues in their self-portraits.

> {Rogers's wrote:
> As regards to the title, Africa's Gift to America, it is fitting to recall, that Africa played a role, perhaps the chief role, in the earliest development of America- a period that antedates Columbus by many centuries, namely Aztec, Maya and Inca Civilizations. About 500A.D. or earlier, Africans sailed over to the Americas and continued to do so until the time of Columbus. This does not call for any particular stretch of the imagination. Africa is only 1600 miles distant from South America with islands in between, among them are St. Paul and Fernando Noronha.} [11]

The Islands in the Atlantic Ocean provided a place for Africans coming to the New World. There were fruit and fish to eat and the island natives were receptive. (This of course was prior to the conquest of Columbus, and other European explorers. They made no difference concerning the status of Africans; all were treated cruelly). In Jackson's book <u>God, Man, and Civilization</u>, he included an article Davidson wrote for the magazine "West Africa," on Saturday, June 7 1969:

> {Jackson wrote concerning Basil Davidson:
> <u>Africans Before Columbus,</u> wrote that Columbus and other early European arrivals in America came back with quite a bit of evidence, suggestive but inclusive, that black peoples from Africa had already reached those shores. Various writers have pointed from time to time, over the past twenty years and more, to the likely West African origins of these black explorers, notably of that tribe of Almamys who were said to have settled in Honduras. }[12]

Slavery was a way of life; according to Bennett in other words it was a long standing tradition. One could be a slave one day, and the next day he or she could become the prime minister, as this form of slavery carried no negative connotations.

> {According to Van Sertima from his book <u>They Came Before Columbus</u>:
> The Indians gave proof that they were trading with black people. They brought to the Spanish concrete evidence of this trade. "The Indians claims of this Espanola said there had come to Espanola a black people who have the tops of their spears made of a metal which they call gua-nin, of which he (Columbus) had sent samples to the Sovereigns to have them assayed, when I was found that of parts, 18 were o gold, 6 of silver and 8 of copper. The origin of the word guanin may be traded down in the Mande languages of West Africa, through Mandingo, Kabunga, Toronka, Kankanka, Bambara, Mande and Vei. In Vei, we have the form of the word ka-ni which transliterated into native phonetics, would give us gua-nin. In Columbus's journal "gold" is given as coa-na, while gua-nin is recorded as an island where there is much gold. } [13]

These metal components were from African tradition only. [1]Espanola or Hispanola, this island is in the West Indies comprising of both the Republic of Haiti and the Dominican Republic. The presence of Blacks with their trading mastery in America, before Columbus, is proven by the representation of Blacks in Native American sculpture and design. Evidentially, the Spanish government passed these laws, as America was not a country at this time in history.

> {Rogers's stated:
> As late as 1650 the South Atlantic was called the Ethiopic, or Ethiopian Ocean, and most of Africa as far as South Africa was called Ethiopia.} [14]

The landmasses might have been closer because the land was joined together in many places where it is no longer joined. The countries were larger landmasses as well. It is not impossible for Africans to be on the various islands or other extended places.

[1]Hispanola, or Espanola were the islands of Haiti and Santa Domingo. Interestingly, enough Dr. Wiener's book <u>Africans and the Discovery of America</u>, Agrees with Van Sertima.

> {Rogers's on Dr. Wiener:
> Professor Wiener, found that these Negro traders traveled as far north as New England. Their relics have been found in graves there, most notably a pipe with Negro face.} [15]

While other writers have eluded to the fact that guanine, a metal from Africa, was found in the New World, which proved that the Africans brought this metals with them. The Black traders from Guinea, who trafficked in a gold alloy, guanin; was made of precisely the same composition and bearing the same name as frequently referred to by other early writers on Africa.

> {Rogers's stated:
> In the fifteenth Century, we find other periodic influxes of Africans in Europe that began under the Pharaohs. They came this time not as conquerors, like the Moors, but as slaves; principally in Portugal and Spain and as far north as England, around 1440 or 1442, some 50 years before the discovery of the New World. Having proved so useful, it was inevitable that the Spaniards would bring them to the New World. } [16]

Dr. Leo Wiener began his research in the early 1920's. Although Africans were later reintroduced to America in slavery, they had preceded Europeans by many hundreds of years. Dr. Wiener's extraordinary research was a three-volume set of books entitled <u>Africa and the Discovery of America</u>. By the late 1920's Dr. Wiener was ridiculed and treated unfairly for his work until he finally left Harvard University.

> {Bennett continues:
> As political entities, Ghana, Mali and Songhay do not suffer in comparison with their European contemporaries. In several areas, in fact, the Sudanese empires were clearly superior. "It would be interesting to know," "what the Normans might have thought of Ghana. Anglo-Saxon England could easily have seemed a poor and lowly place beside it."} [17]

It seems that Africa was far more advanced compared to other known worlds. This high civilization was well noted by the Greeks, and because of them we now know of their accomplishments.

Africans were travelers, and traders and well-established businessmen, long before the European invasion.

> {Rogers's continues with Count Volney:
> Two thousand years later another famous traveler, Count Volney, said on his visit to Egypt in 1787, that what Herodotus said had solved for him the problem of why the people were so Negroid in appearance an especially the Great Sphinx of Ghizeh, supreme symbol of worship and power. Reflecting on the them state of the Egyptians compared with what they had been, he said, "To think that to a race of black men who are today our slaves and the object of our contempt is the same one to whom we owe our arts, sciences and even the very use of speech."} [18]

The dark people's appearance rather than others often judged their abilities and talents, as was the case with early Egyptians. Amazingly some of the civil and religious systems still govern the United States of America and other first World nations came from the Black group.

{Rogers's continues with his research with Count Volney:
States, of the blacks he saw in Upper Egypt among the ruins of the colossal monuments there, he said, "There a people now forgotten discovered while others were yet barbarians, the elements of the arts and science. A race of men now rejected from society for their sable skin and wooly hair, founded on the study of the laws of nature those civil and religious systems which still govern the universe." } [19]

It seems clear that for hundreds or perhaps thousands of years Africans and their contributions were deleted from the annals of the world's history books.

{Rogers's wrote that J.G. Jackson writing in 1809 stated:
They, (the Moors) carried the Christian captives (mainly Whites) about the desert to the different Markets to sell them for they soon discovered, that their habits of life render them unserviceable, or very inferior to the black slaves from Timbuctoo. After traveling three days to one market, five to another, nay, sometimes fourteen, they at length become objects of commercial speculation and the itinerant Jew traders, who wander about Wedinoon to sell their wares find means to barter them for tobacco, salt, a cloth garment, or any other thing.} [20]

Bennett stated that all men from all backgrounds have been enslaved at some point over history. Color has intentionally been the primary focus for abuse from Europeans, and their hatred of the Africans. Early traders and foreigners did not seem to be troubled by trading with Africans. The distinction between one skin color and another was not significant during this period in history. The skin tone of a person did not indicate one's race or ethnic origin; but perhaps the clothing one wore spoke to the status one held. Europeans used religion to justify their exploitation of people of color, including Africans and Native Americans. Europeans felt it necessary to "save the heathens" by introducing them to Christianity.

However, much of Africa had already known Christianity; especially because the first man made in God's own image existed very near or in Africa itself. This world was once just a large mass of land, where all the people were the same and spoke the same language.

Rogers's continues by adding a statement that concurs with Wagener's Pangia Theory, which states that the earth was once a large landmass, which occurred much earlier in history. The Pangia Theory suggests that the volcanic eruptions and the movement of the tectonic plates led to the separation of the land into sections. Africans and Europeans seemingly had a good trade relationship.

Africans led the way for world trading and were treated as equals or, should it be said, they were treated as kings and dignitaries prior to the conquest of Columbus. In fact, Rogers's said Columbus received information about the Americas from Africans in Spain and Portugal prior to his "discovery" of America. They reported riches and wonderful things were to be found in [1]Espanola.

{According to Rogers's Dr. Wiener concludes:
Africa and the Discovery of America, he gives abundant proof that they were. He says, "The presence of Negroes before Columbus is proved by the representation of Negroes in American sculpture and design; by the occurrence of a black nation at Darien[2] early in the 16th Century and more specifically by Columbus' empathic reference to Negro traders from Guinea (Ghana), who trafficked in gold alloy of precisely the same composition and bearing the same name (Guanin), is frequently referred to by early writers on Africa. } [21]

The presence of Blacks with their trading mastery in America, before Columbus, is proven by the representation of Blacks in Native American sculpture and design. Evidentially, the Spanish government passed these laws, as America was not a country at this time in history.

1
2   Darien is an arm of the Caribbean between NE Panama and NW Columbia. It is the former name for the Isthmus of Panama. Actually Africans were then re-introduced to America in slavery for many hundreds or thousands of years, prior they had been in the Western Hemisphere.

In fact Rogers stated that Columbus received information from Africans that were in Spain and Portugal prior to his "discovery" of America.

> {Rogers's stated:
> C.C. Marquez says, "The Negro type is seen in the most ancient Mexican sculpture…Negro type figures were found frequently in the most remote tradition." Riva Palacio, a Mexican historian says "it is indisputable that in very ancient times the Negro race occupied our territory (Mexico) when the two continents were joined. The Mexicans recall a Negro god, Ixilton, which means 'black face.'"}….[22]

Author's note: Please take another look at the cover of this book, the face it that of the Black god Ixilton from Mexico.

> {Continuing with Rogers concerning N. Leon:
> "The almost extinction of the original Negroes during the time of the Spanish conquest and the memories of them in the most ancient traditions induce us to believe that the Negroes were the first inhabitants of Mexico.} [23]

The Olmecs (an early people) from Mexico worshipped a god they called Ixilton, which was a black-faced gigantic head with African features, and tight curled hair. The people were dark that inhabited Mexico in ancient history. (This is in agreement with Van Sertima's, book They Came Before Columbus).

Old maps were very beneficial in providing the names of the Oceans and certain locations on maps that were made at an earlier period in history. The term White with all of its arrogance was not heard of until after the 17th Century.

However, whites had no conception of being white, or it lacked importanceearly on in hsitory. Research has shown that in earlier periods in history, Whites did not seem to think very much of their skin color. The majority of people with whom they dealt were persons of color, and it did not seem to matter.

Legal documents from the time identified Whites as Englishmen or Christians. The word "white," with its burden of arrogance and biological pride, developed late in the century as a direct result of European instigation.

Historically, the word "white" was used for the most part in reference to clothing or other items surrounding a person; not the color of skin. Van Sertima said the word white was a purely European invention when used as an exclusive reference for skin color or race. "White" in American Indian terms did not mean a color for humans in pre-Columbian times. Van Sertima asserted the Natives further thought of Quetzalcoatl as being a god when he first came to shore from a boat. [Possibly because he was wearing white garments}.

> The truth is "white" is purely an European convention when used as an exclusive referent for skin color and race. Quetzalcoatl did not have Northern Europeans features. Native Americans spoke of him at times as being white in a symbolic sense, in the way Muslims may speak of Mohammed as a handful of white light in Allah's palm. A black or brown Negroid Hamitic man, as Abubakari was, appearing out of the east in long flowing white Muslim robes would be called white. } [24]

At this period in history "color" did not seem to have the same significance as in recent years. For example: Egyptians painted in their caves and made colored paintings, whenever people were depicted they were always other colors except for "white." There are many speculations concerning this phenomenon, however, suffice it to say that somehow three-fourths of the world is of color and only one-fourth is considered to be Caucasian. Clothing sometimes represented whether a person was belonged to one group or another.

History has been called "his-story," because Europeans were writing history; and of course they would shed great light on their accomplishments. {Even if they had stolen the discoveries from others}. As the European developed skills for recording information it seems likely that they wrote as if all discoveries came from them. Noting here that

Africans and others used a form of recording by word of mouth history was passed on called the 'oral traditions.' Egyptians always saw themselves as being colored. It is understandable that they were proud of their color, as they should have been.

Dr. Leo Wiener began his studies in the early 1900's. Although Africans were later re-introduced to America in slavery, they had preceded Europeans by many hundreds of years. Dr. Wiener's extraordinary research was a three-volume set of books entitled _Africa and the Discovery of America_. Dr. Wiener was treated very poorly and was often ridiculed and taunted for his findings.

(This author' notes: Bigotry and inhumanity was utilized by some professors while Dr. Wiener was a Professor at Harvard University in the 1920's).

Professor Wiener found that African traders traveled as far north into the Americas as New England. Their relics have been found in graves such as a "pipe with a Negro face." These relics were undeniably African in origin. Dr. Wiener believed Africans had brought these relics when they crossed the ocean via a land bridge or boat. This and more information can be found in his book Africa and the Discovery of America. Africans were very talented and ingenious in that they were able to make things that many wondered how it was possible.

Africans have never been given credit for many of their contributions to the world; nor were they given credit for their many inventions in America. Most people do not know of the contributions made during, after, and to this day by African Americans. (This author listed just a few in the conclusion of the book).

Africans also made large boats with many floors and elaborate trim, often in gold. Van Sertima stated that Thor Heyerdahl believed the Africans were capable of making reed boats or rafts that could sail the Atlantic.

Van Sertima explores Thor Hyderdahl the Norwegian writer and explorer actually set out to examine the claims of the rafts and small boats crossing the Atlantic Ocean. This gave the needed validity to claims that Africans had indeed traversed the Oceans.

{Hyderdahl's voyages:
With Buduma tribesmen under the direction of Abdullah Dji-brine, a papyrus expert from Lake Chad, a replica of the ancient papyrus boat was built. Heyerdahl called this the Ra, the word for sun in ancient Egypt as well as in parts of America and on all the islands of Polynesia. The Ra I set out from Safi, on the Atlantic coast of North Africa, on May 25, 1969. It sailed to within a few days of the New World before it got into serious trouble. The Heyerdahl expedition had made one mistake. In the Egyptian model a rope ran down from the curved tip of the stern to the afterdeck. It was thought that this roe was only there to maintain the curve of the stern. In fact the stern, through this rope, acted as a spring supporting the pliant afterdeck. The ill-advised removal of this rope caused the afterdeck to sag, and the boat listed dangerously as it neared Barbados. } [25]

This first voyage made the news and people were amazed that a raft could make such a long and difficult voyage; the fact that it only reached the islands did not seem to matter.

{Heyerdahl's exploits continue:
A smaller model, Ra II, built on the identical Egyptian pattern by a Native American tribe, the Aymara, who profited from this trial and error, made it across the Atlantic from Africa necessary. What Heyerdahl had proven, in effect, was the most ancient of Egyptian ships, predecessors of even more sophisticated models, could have crossed the Atlantic. He demonstrated also, through the shipbuilding labors of the Buduma tribesmen, that these navigational skills had been largely *preserved among Riverine and Lacustrine Africans even to the present day. The papyrus boat however is but a modest curtain raiser on the vast theater of ancient* Egyptian shipping. } [26]

Many issues arose due to the fact that the native's advice was not followed in the building of the RA I. However, they listened to the Ayamaras when building the RA II and the journey was successful all the way into the Western Hemisphere.

Many people have speculated that Africans were "landlocked" and thus not able to navigate the waters that surround their continent. (This author visited Africa and actually saw children swimming the Atlantic Ocean). Most Africans learn to swim in lakes, rivers and the ocean, and are magnificent swimmers. They learn to swim early as a matter of survival and scholars have long speculated that a great seafaring nation once existed on Africa's west coast and they sent ships to the Americas.

Many Europeans do not want to know about the early development in Egypt or any parts of Africa. They made consorted efforts to erase these facts from the pages of history to keep them pristine and white at any cost.

Africans gave the world marvelous inventions, many of which are still in present use. These are two large cities in Africa: Gambia and Sierra Leone. Africa has provided food plants that are used in America even today. Africans have contributed to the World and to the Americas.

Africans and their presence was evident and written down in the records of Mexico. This is true of Columbus; on his third voyage he stated that he saw Negroes.

Rogers's continues with his research on early slavery in Europe: (Author's note: When the years of the 1400's are taken into account the figure of over 430 years emerges for the New World slavery, almost identical time that the Israelites were under slavery in Egypt).

(Author's note: Columbus was setting sail for India in the east therefore, when he arrived in the west instead of east the Natives he encountered he called "Indians)."

{Van Sertima continues:
The African presence in America before Columbus is of importance not only to African and American history but also to the history of world civilizations. It provides further evidence the al great civilizations races are heavily indebted to one another and

that no race has a monopoly on enterprises and inventive genius.

Stone heads proves the African presence; terra cottas, skeletons, artifacts, techniques and inscriptions prove the African presence, by oral traditions and documented history, by botanical, linguistic and cultural data. When the feasibility of African crossings of the Atlantic was not proven and the archaeological evidence undated and unknown, we could in all innocence ignore the most startling of coincidences. This is no longer possible. The case for African contacts with pre-Columbian America, in spite of a number of understandable gaps and a few minor elements of contestable data, is no longer based on the fanciful conjecture and speculation of romantics. It is grounded now upon an overwhelming and growing body of reliable witnesses. Using Dr. Rhine's dictum or phenomena that were once questionable but are now being empirically confirmed, truly it may be said: The overwhelming incidence of coincidence argues overwhelmingly against a mere coincidence. } [27]

This from Van Sertima sums up the materials that were included in this section to show the many contributions and inventions provided to the world by Africans. The contributors to this book were multicultural from many diverse backgrounds. Having been presented from various people with diverse backgrounds helped to inspire this book; and the agreement that was compiled was of utmost importance. There is also evidence to show that African Americans have contributed to the inventions and ingenious devices made available to America. The New World had so many artifacts from Africa that it is very difficult to deny how they arrived at such locations. It seems that men from various educational fields of study with credible credentials now authenticate early expeditions by Africans.

There are many myths surrounding Africa this author has chosen just a few:
- Africa nurtured a landlocked race of people
- Africa had no knowledge of lands not connected to her
- Africa never had any mariners
- African's never constructed boats

- Africa's empires ended at the edge of the desert
- Africa is unwashed by the world's seas

These myths are found in history books as well as other historical sources, and this book has dismantled most of these myths J.A. Rogers's continues:

"Africans were navigating the Atlantic before Christ."

Rogers's and Wiener concur that Africans were a sea faring group. Interestingly enough, Dr. Leo Wieners discoveries were never disproven neither were Dr. L.S. B. Leakey's many findings, or Joel Augustus Rogers's; (he wrote over twelve books on Africans and African Americans) to date none have been disputed, Ivan Van Sertima's works are also held in high esteem. These are just a few of the many authors, historians, researchers, philogists, archeologists, educators, and scientific scholars.

Africans have a place in history, as they have contributed to world civilizations as well as to American history. However, it was the Greeks who gave written proof that traced the African contributions back to antiquity. Africa is a very large continent and it dates back to biblical days.

Africa is made up of over 50 countries with people speaking over 2,500 languages and dialects; they also have different cultures and customs from one country to the other. Centuries of contact and interbreeding have already produced different looking Africans. Some West Africans were short and broad-nosed some were tall with straight hair and aquiline noses. Africans are all colors: chocolate, asphalt, café au lait, persimmon, and cream. (Note: This definition comes from Lerone Bennett, Jr.~ these descriptions are so nice, I wish I could have claimed it for myself). In other words Black hues encompass all shades from "Ebony to Ivory" like Stevie Wonder stated.

Blacks, like any other people, look different from one another. Subtle variations occur from region to region. Evidently, to some European scholars, there were no differences at all. Africans were all treated the same, no matter how important some of the dignitaries might have been (a king or queen was treated without respect for their former positions or status). The main characteristic apparent to Europeans was their Black skin. The only "equality" these slavers practiced was a parity of bigotry, and unbridled cruelty toward those they sought to subjugate, dehumanize, and treat like chattel property; this was the plight of the African when he was re-introduced to the Americas and the Western Hemisphere!

Judge not, that ye be not judged.
-Matthew 7:1

Chapter IV.
The Social Significance of race and ethnicity:

Sociology, a new science created in the nineteenth century, had its roots steeped in European thought and behavior. This discipline proposes to be the scientific, empirical research of man in various group interactions and behavior. For example, this manuscript will concentrate on "race and ethnicity" as it relates to sociology.

{The Sociology of race and ethnicity according to Macionis: "Race: is a category composed of men and women who share biologically transmitted traits that are defined as socially significant. Races are commonly distinguished by physical traits such as skin color, hair texture, shape of facial features, and body type. Racial diversity appeared among our human ancestors as the result of living in different geographical regions of the world. Members of a single biological species, human beings display biological variations—described as "racial characteristics" In regions of intense heat, for example, humans developed darker skin (from the natural pigment, melanin) as protection from the sun; in regions with moderate climates, people have lighter skin. Skin tone differences are-literally-only skin deep because every human being the world over is a member of a single biological species." } [1]

However, early in European history a mind-set of superiority evolved that permeated the entire world. One of the most fearsome examples of this would be Hitler's ideology of death and destruction towards anyone who wasn't Aryan during the era when his maniacal Nazi regime was in power in Germany. This was the beginning of modern "racism." The idea that one group of people was "superior" to another became more common practice, especially in America.

Social scientists in Europe decided anthropology would be the "vehicle" that would place Europeans above all other groups. They made up the guidelines, naturally writing in favor of their features and characteristics. This was the beginning of an educational system and the superiority complex of the Aryan group. Sociologists of today, as a group, tend not to adhere to any such notion nor do they tend to give any platform for this line of reasoning. The distinctions and variations between human groups came about for many reasons, unrelated to the inferiority of some groups or the superiority of others nineteenth century biologists studying the world's racial diversity developed a three-part typology.

> {Also from Macionis:
> They made three classifications of humanity. The people with lighter skin and finer softer hair were called Caucasian; the people with darker skin and coarser hair, Negroid; and the people with yellow or brown skin and distinctive folds on their eyelids, Mongoloid. } [2]

We know from the movement of humans from all ends of the earth there had been intermarriage, and intermixing for many hundreds of years, therefore, there is only one conclusion to come to and that is humans are all from the same beginnings and the same family. Homo sapiens or mankind are what we are; not descendents from animals but made after the image of the Almighty God and His son Jesus.

Most notably in the United States it seems the "race" has far reaching implications, and the notion that one group is better than another is still believed by some even in the twenty-first century. Most American Caucasians have some Negroid genes, and the same hold true for the African American, most will have some Caucasian ancestry.

No matter the reality of mixed groups in America, people are quick to rank and classify each other racially as belonging to one group or the other. There is no scientific research that supports such assertions, as one group is inherently "better" than another. In the southern states a person with a "drop of Negro blood" was considered to be an African American. Today, however, with less caste distinctions in America, the law allows parents to declare the race of a child as they wish.

This author prays for the day that we will no longer have boxes that ask what race one happens to be, that the only choices will be American or non-American. The division of groups is very divisive.

{Macionis states:
The 1990 census forms shows that more than 10 million people described themselves by checking more than one racial category. }[3]

Hopefully, as time goes on race will become less important in American society and in the world.

{Macionis continues: (Note: All of the definitions were taken from Macionis:

"Ethnicity is a shared cultural heritage. Members of an ethnic category have common ancestors, language, or religions, which, together, confer a distinctive social identity."} [4]

Ethnicity is a far better example than race, simply because it involves more variety, culture, languages and a people's way of life.

{This author has alluded that the most criminal of all words "racism," the definition is:

"A powerful and destructive form of prejudice, racism refers to the belief that one racial category is innately superior or inferior to another."} [5]

Racism has been widespread in America for centuries. Ideas about the inferiority of race gave credence to slavery and the bondage of humans for hundreds of years; because of an illogical notion. Today, overt racism is far less identifiable than in previous years, mainly due to the egalitarian culture that urges us to evaluate all people, "not by the color of their skin but by the content of their character." From the late Rev./Dr. Martin Luther King, Jr. However, racism is still "alive and well" in many sections of the United States. Racism is a sickness of the mind that affects the behavioral systems of some people and, to a greater or lesser degree, extends itself throughout all of American society.

It is not unscholarly to say that these racist policies began in the European mind-set. This is a very dangerous ideology that has been used for man to justify committing inhumane acts upon his fellow man. It is a strong reason why our history is so filled with violence.

Sociologists are scientific in their approach to race and ethnicity and tend to present factual information without regard for any one particular belief system as being better or worse than another. In other words America was founded on the Bible and its Holy scriptures, however, through the years America evolved into a slave holding nation of the sixteenth and part of the eighteenth centuries. It seemed that the Europeans were fleeing Europe to have religious freedoms, only to enslave a free people from Africa solely because of their color and the need for laborers to build this nation. The laws in America soon declared that all Africans were to be legally held in bondage perpetually.

President Abraham Lincoln wrote the Emancipation Proclamation, in 1862, and it became law to free the slaves. This was Jan 1, 1863, all the slave states near Washington, D.C., were set free. But, it was as late as June 1865, when the slaves were free in the distant states like Texas, therefore, the celebration of "Juneteenth." This is a celebration once per year on Jun 19th to celebrate freedom from slavery. There is much fun and singing, games, African American art, handmade items, tee shirts, and soul food to share. Most cities throughout America have them and it is a positive event to attend for all groups.

Chapter V.

The Re-introduction of Blacks to the Americas (1400's-1865)

Africans sailed over to the Americas is surrounding islands, on rafts and small boats. They populated many of the islands and mixed with the Native Americans in this land that we now call America. All was peaceful; people of different ethnicities co-existing with one another. This went on for hundreds of years, prior to Columbus sailing over to "find a land that was already inhabited with people." He did not "discover" anything; a land inhabited by people cannot be discovered, they were never lost to begin with. Columbus was lost; he was headed for India, and trying to reach the east by sailing west. He mistakenly called the Natives he found in the New World "Indians."

Based on the ancient code of war, African slavery depended on the victor of a battle. Losing armies were enslaved, yet slaves were given every opportunity to coexist with their captors; to work, to live, and to prosper without any stigma attached to their servitude, especially not a color one.

American slavery was the opposite; this was one of the most barbarous and horrific slave practices in modern times. Slaves were in the New World throughout a period of close to 430 years. Africans were maimed, raped, and murdered on a wholesale basis. Over 100 million were taken from Africa to be enslaved, according to the *Original Black Heritage Study Bible;* however, the exact number is unknown. Taking Africans from Africa began as early as the 1400's.

> {Franklin & Moss stated:
> When in 1517, Bishop Bartolomo de las Casas advocated the encouragement of immigration to the New World by permitting Spaniards to import African slaves, the trading of me in the New World formally began. Las Casas was so determined to relieve Indians of the onerous burden of slavery that he recommended the enslavement of Africans. (Later, he so deeply regretted having taken this position that he vigorously renounced it.)} [1]

All Africans were not content to be slaves, many led insurrections. There were many slave revolts, but few were written about, including Denmark Vesey, Gabriel Prosser, Nat Turner, and John Brown, the famous White insurrectionist at Harper's Ferry, VA.

African familial ties were based on kinship within ethnic groups or tribes. Under American slavery, Blacks weren't grouped along any family lines; they were individually tagged and identified. In other words, the sense of family or community was gone, and the mutual concern for each other, as it had been in Africa, was denied. In some aspects, this kinship closeness seems to be missing in the African-American group to this day.

> {According to Horne:
> The large, lightly populated land was the main reason for slavery, based upon the Europeans' greed. No man needs more land than he can farm successfully alone; this policy maintains a natural balance of things. However, the need for more and more land was the primary method for becoming wealthy and powerful, regardless of the upheaval it caused to Native Americans or African slaves. } [2]

Greed was the primary reason for the importing of Africans into slavery. The ownership of great quantities of land tended to lead to power and thus a great deal of wealth.

{Horne continues:
This was the European justification for the mass exodus of Africans being re-introduced into the Americas. Because European plantation owners were greedy for land, it was necessary to travel over 8,000 miles to capture and enslave a free people. Black people were also identifiable as slaves and could not blend into the fabric of the European society taking form in America. The battle cry in the new land was for religious freedom and equality but these equalities and freedoms were limited to a select ethnic group. The very rights that Europeans had fled from Europe to seek in the Americas were denied to African slaves. The landowners needed "free, slave labor" to harvest their crops. Even converting to Christianity had no bearing on the way slaves were treated by their "masters."} [3]

The large plantations provided the opportunity for these "Christians" to import African from Africa via thievery. The Churches were supporters of human bondage. Even converting to Christianity was no guarantee of better treatment as was promised. There were some ministers like John Wesley (a Caucasian) that fought against slavery but he was in the minority along with a few others that hated slavery, and would later become Abolitionists.

{From Superman to Man by J. A. Rogers's:
Darwin in his 'Descent of Man,' says that when the Negro boys on the east coast of Africa saw Burton, the explorer, they cried out: 'Look at the white man, he looks like a white ape.' The unsophisticated African entertains an aversion to white people, and when accidentally or unexpectedly meeting a white man, he turns and takes to his heels. It is because he feels that he has come upon some unusual or unearthly creature, some hobgoblin or ghost or sprite, and that an aquiline nose, scant lips, and cat-like eyes afflict him.} [4]

"The Yoruba word for white man is not complimentary. It means 'peeled man.' Stanley, the explorer, said that when he returned from the wilds of Africa he found the complexions of Europeans ghastly 'after so long gazing on rich black and richer bronze.'"

Slavery and the theft of millions of Africans from Africa shocked and frightened the people of Africa. Many had never seen a "White" person before; it was strange to see the 'pale' skin color. This author visited the slave castles on Ghana's coast, and saw the two large castles are El Mina, and Cape Coast. The original holding places still exist, and the famous 'door of no return' was also there. A plaque was placed over the portal stating that once you pass through you will not be able to return. This author felt the dread that those earlier Africans must have felt. And I knew that I was coming out of the dungeon.

The feeling was grim and dismal even for any tourist to experience. This must have been a very horrific event for the newly captured Africans, to be torn from their life to face the unknown. There were the eerie sounds of the Atlantic Ocean beating upon the rocks surrounding the castles this had a bone chilling effect. This author attempted to explore these caves and circumstances for the classes I taught, however, no matter what I thought I could do I was unable to focus as my imagination took me back hundreds of years and I too was one of the captives. My dedication to filming the exact cave and its interior happened with closed eyes I could hear crying, wailing, and so much sadness so profound that it felt as if one could reach out and touch the throngs of people. (This author was in tears as were other tourists from various countries throughout the world).

This was a real firsthand look at the reality of slavery. It was a very emotionally and spiritually draining day for this educator. We had a tour leader who was rather matter of fact about all the things that happened there those many years before. Interestingly enough the upstairs was the living quarters for the captains and the crew. There was also a Church of sorts where they prayed to God, while human carnage was in the hole hewn out of the rock below that housed men, women and children. To make money the Ghanaian Government had lights installed into the caves and added a few steps, for tourists. The Africans were merely thrown into the hole. There were tiny holes at the top of the caves that provided what air and light if any that they had. It was an awful example of man's inhumanity towards his fellow-man. I pray that this sort of brutality is never repeated!

However, if there was a young pretty woman they were held separately in other rooms and the men used them for sex slaves while awaiting the next ship. If by chance they became pregnant, they were set free, if not they were taken along with the rest of the Africans to become slaves in the New World. Author's feelings and opinions are included. Note: No matter what language some Africans spoke, there were others from other areas that spoke a different dialect or language; however, they were expected to understand one another, when the only common thread that held them together was the hue of their skin. The main common means of communication was the playing of the drums; it was a method of alerting the people when danger was near. The usage of drums was stopped shortly after arriving in America. Later while teaching classes on African slavery this author had a very different slant from a very realistic and personal touch. I advised all of my students that if the opportunity presented itself that they too should take a trip to the slave castles in Accra, Ghana.

{According to Bennett:
…The -European slave trade – began in 1444 and continued for more than 400 years. During this period, Africa lost an estimated forty million people. Some twenty million of these men and women came to the New World. Millions more died in Africa during and after their capture or on the ships and plantations…. The slave trade was people living, lying, stealing, murdering and dying. The slave trade was a black man who stepped out of his hut for a breath of fresh air and ended up, ten months later, in Georgia with bruises on his back and a brand on his chest. The slave trade was black mother suffocating her newborn baby because she didn't want him to grow up a slave.} [5]

Other experts have suggested that over one hundred million slaves were taken and at least half were lost at sea on the long voyage in such dilapidated conditions.

Africans had to reconnect to their own religion, which was yet another human dignity that had been denied to them; so they met late at night, usually by the riverside, and prayed for freedom and begged God to intercede on their behalf. The slave masters went so far as to take away their languages, dialects and other traditions the slaves needed to remain connected with each other. They were subject to their owners and treated worse than the animals the owner had on his large plantation.

The first slaves were Native Americans. However, they escaped or resisted, preferring to even die of starvation rather than be enslaved. Many Africans did the same; several attempted to jump ship in an attempt to swim back to Africa. Hundreds perhaps even thousands, died in transit by various means. The slave ships stopped in the islands so that the Masters could "break their spirits; by lashing and telling them how to behave." Overseers killed slaves for various infractions once they reached America.

It has been estimated that about 30 percent of the Blacks put on ship in Africa died crossing the Atlantic, it being a common practice to throw the sick overboard. Probably half the survivors died soon after reaching America because of the strange food and disease for which they had built up no immunity.

{Gerald Horne stated:

Millions of men, women, and children died on the Middle Passage. The cause of this was not, as the texts often imply, suicide, or spoiled food, or homesickness, but epidemics due to foul water, overcrowding, filthy and unsanitary conditions, not to mention beatings and murders to set an example. The point that the texts neglect in lamenting these "losses" is that this wastage was predictable, and figured quite rationally upon the account books of the merchants who conducted the trade.} [6]

It seemed that slaves had no choice in anything that affected their lives. They had no privacy and no control over their lives or their family members lives. Everything was according to the master and his decisions.

John G. Jackson said that millions Africans were taken from the African continent. The writers of <u>the Original African Heritage Study Bible</u> agree with Jackson.

{According to Jackson from <u>Introduction to African Civilization</u> he stated:
All told, the slave trade was responsible for the deaths of over one hundred million Africans.} [7]

The White slave masters were not concerned with the losses of slaves on the voyage, as their profits would be great enough without attempting to save them all. The slaves were thought to be inexhaustible; therefore, no mercy or pity was shown to slaves no matter the plight. Slaves were the property "in all that entails" of the Europeans owners. They felt that the Africans would never run out, and it slavery would continue forever.

Europeans (generally those of lowest rank and outcasts) were also brought from the Old World as indentured slaves from the streets and over-crowed prisons. They were prostitutes, thieves, murderers, religious heretics and homeless citizens. These Caucasian slaves easily escaped and blended into the free European society. The indentured slaves who worked out their sentences were often emancipated with a piece of land and a little money to begin their lives anew. So much for the upstanding Europeans with the Christian perspective for this new country!

Ironically, very little has ever been written concerning European indentured slaves. There were many in the beginning; however, they were not very strong or durable and would often run away. This posed a large problem for the masters; they had to find a way to get laborers and insure they would have strong workers. Some crewmembers had seen the farms and workers off the coast of Africa in their travels. African slaves were the ideal solution to the conundrum.

In 1619, Africans were re-introduced to the New World as indentured servants at first, along with Europeans. Servitude was also a method of payment for the expense of the trip from Europe and Africa to the Americas. However, Whites after spending their servitude time were released, with some money and a piece of land. The status of Africans being held as an indentured slave lasted from 1619 until about 1661; then changes were implemented to debase and subject the Black slave to a lifetime of degradation. The Virginia colonists introduced the idea of "lifetime" or perpetual slavery in the late 1600's. Once it became law in Virginia, other southern states soon followed suit. Slavery was soon converted into perpetual or lifelong rather than having an end date. The state of Virginia was the state that introduced lifelong or slavery for life. Slavery was an unimaginably barbaric practice – especially by people who took pride in claiming the name of "Christian." Many Christians owned slaves, and some were cruel to their slaves as were the non- Christians.

{According to Franklin & Moss:
Slave breeding, strangely enough, was one of the most approved methods of increasing agriculture capital. The traditional slave trade was castigated b the slave holding gentry as being inhumane, vicious, and extremely venal; but slave breeding was far more common and much more highly esteemed in the community. One respectable Virginia planter boasted that his women were "uncommonly good breeders" and that he never heard of babies coming as fast as they did on his plantation. Of course, the very gratifying thing about it was that 'every one of them was worth two hundred dollars…the moment they drew breath.' Indeed, breeding was so profitable that many slave girls became mothers at thirteen and fourteen years of age. By the time they were twenty, some young women have given birth to as many as five children. Bounties and prizes were offered for great prolificacy, ad in some instances, freedom was granted to mothers who had enriched their masters to the extent of bearing them ten to fifteen children. } [8]

Slave breeding was carried on with such indifference to the woman's health or any physical conditions that pregnancy might have caused. All that mattered was that the baby was to be sold. At times women were forced to work in the fields very soon after having given birth.

{According to Jesse Bernard:
Women could love children conceived under such circumstances is, in a way quite remarkable, yet many of them were fiercely maternal. "The old overseer, he hat my many, 'cause she fight him for beating her children. Why, she git more "whupppings" for that than anything else." Even the children of hated White fathers were cherished. "She was so glad freedom come on before her children come on old enough to sell." Part-White children sold for more money than unmixed Black children.} 9

A slave mother's love is a hard thing to explain, the children were loved no matter their origin. There were also times when a woman would not cut the umbilical cord and the baby would die, the mother would rather the child died than to have to grow up to be a slave and suffer its entire life. Slavery was perpetual, and there seemed to be no way of escaping its grasp!

In 1712, Willie Lynch proposed methods for the plantation owners to control their slaves. He wrote, "I use fear, distrust and envy for control purposes. These methods worked throughout my plantation in the West Indies and it will work throughout the South....

{I assure you that distrust is stronger than trust, and envy is stronger than adulation, respect or admiration." [From a copy of The Willie Lynch Document written in 1712] On the top of Lynch' list came age, followed by: "color" or shade, intelligence, stature, sex, the size of the plantation, status and attitude of the master, whether the slaves lived in a valley, hill, the direction of their residence; whether they had fine or coarse hair or were tall or short. } 10

Imagine how difficult it is for an intelligent person to hear Blacks calling each other names, most of those derogatory words were used at lynching's; such as the word n.....! No doubt the word for lynching came from Willie Lynches' name. Other put downs and negative names all suggest an internalized mentality for some people of color. This is a very sad state of affairs, and Blacks need to understand how detrimental it is to use such deadly words towards each other.

> {Lynch continues:
> The Black slave, after receiving this indoctrination shall carry on and will become self-debasing and will perpetuate these negatives for hundreds of years, maybe even thousands. }

After one hundred and forty-six years the negativity continues, this is a very sad but truthful commentary on some African Americans or Blacks.

> {Lynch went on to say:
> Slave owners must pit the young against the old slaves, and use skin tone against them. "Color has always proven to be problematic for the slaves," he said.

Unfortunately this is still true today for some African Americans cannot stand to see those of their group with fair skin and softer hair. The adages from Lynch still permeate some African American communities; it has lessened now that Miss American can be an African American of a darker hue; without having to look almost white.

With this kind of indoctrination it is no wonder there are multiple problems within the African-American community even to this very day. In modern times these feelings of so-called "being close to White" is not in vogue, and all shades of African Americans are now treated the same. It was refreshing however, to see a very dark-skinned Miss America, after beautiful Vanessa Williams who was fair with her green eyes, and soft hair. Vanessa Williams, you are true beauty, but my point still needed to have been made.

There were also inter-marriages between Whites and Africans. These marriages did not seem to be ostracized by other Whites in the area, at first. In the beginning, only male Africans were brought to the

Americas. Later, it was decided that African women should be imported so that Black males could mate with their "own kind." In contrast, interracial marriages-particularly between European men and African women-were common, sanctioned, and encouraged in Latin America, even under slavery.

> {According to Ivan Van Sertima:
> Nicholas Leon, an eminent Mexican authority, reports on the oral traditions of the Native Americans, according to some of who "the oldest inhabitants of Mexico were Negroes."} [11]

Africans traveled the world and it seems that they left their artifacts as reminders of their having been in various places. Scientists have proven that the human DNA is 98% the same for all groups of people.

There is no such thing as a "race," that is a man-made term without any real validity. White males had the ability to do whatever they desired to the Black slave woman because he was the law. The Black woman and her husband (or man) had no recourse; they were powerless to protect themselves or their children. While some White masters would sell their bi-racial offspring, others would keep and free their children upon their deaths; and often leave them land, houses and money. That is how many Blacks after slavery were able to have a positive start toward becoming self- sufficient. (Author's note: There were always free men in America during slavery; they managed to escape to Canada or to other northern states that did not uphold slavery).

Mr. Bill Drayton is a friend of mine. He lives in Christchurch, Dorsett, in the United Kingdom. I came across his article on the Internet, and he gave me his permission on December seventh to add portions of his article into my book. Born and raised in England, Mr. Drayton has written an article on his past family in America. He knows some of his Black relatives. Drayton on this recent trip to Charleston, South Carolina where he will hopefully see relatives some that he has not met before. Bill Drayton is very proud of his relatives of 'color.'

The Grimke-Drayton's:
Mr. Drayton's article about his American genealogy: (Internet)

The Drayton's first settled in the Carolina colony in 1679. They became one of the wealthiest plantation-owning families, with 30 properties. The Grimke's' arrived in the early 18th century," he wrote. His great-great-great-great aunts, Sarah and Angeline Grimke, campaigned against slavery and for women's rights.
After the death of his first wife, their brother Henry Grimke took Nancy Weston, one of his slaves, as his wife in an illegal, mixed marriage. Together, they had three sons; Archibald, Francis and John.

Archibald was involved in law and politics, whereas Francis became a Presbyterian minister in Washington, D.C. Both fought for equal rights for all. It seemed that all the children grew up to be successful in life. } [12]

This is but one example from slavery, however, most Black women were still obligated to serve their White masters as though they never had any children for them. Often, the master would impregnate his wife and a Black slave about the same time so the slave could wet-nurse for the White woman. It was considered unsightly for proper White women to suckle their children and many were too weak after childbirth to care for their infants. Instead of nursing and coddling her own baby, the slave had to provide the White child with nurture. The slave woman was trusted with a new White life, but could not be a mother to her own babies.

What an upside-down state of affairs! Blacks were not good enough to be considered to be human however they were good enough to nurse and care for the master's children, and most could not read or write. Actually the Black slave women breast-fed the babies of their owners. (Note: Slaves had to give medications to the family and children often, also they prepared their food). That is an enormous amount of pressure on the female slave; to try to get the medicines correct and prepare the food without knowing how much of anything to use in preparation. Black works have been well-known however, not the identity of the Blacks responsible for them. For instance:

{Rogers's <u>from Superman to Man</u> he stated:

…When the two races meet in Europe each of the people in question can learn something ennobling from the other, an ennobling influence has no color. When a Caucasian reads Terence, Aesop, Dumas, Pushkin, Georgie Douglas John and Jesse Fauset; admires the paintings of Tanner, Scott or Harper; or listen to the music of Coleridge-Taylor, Rosamond Johnson, Dett or Burleigh, has associates with what for a better name we will call Negro Thought. If one has association with author's works than why not give credit to the authors (ethnicities) themselves?} [13]

Historically, this information is barely known because most people have been taught that these were Europeans of distinguished nobility.

(In this author's opinion if some of these persons had common names like Smith or Williams one would wonder if their climb to fame would have so undaunted). Most books declare Pushkin to be Russian, Dumas a darker skinned European; much like a Clark Gable and Aesop to be a Greek mentor. They could and would be described as anything but what they were people of <u>African descent</u>. There was a time in ancient history that marriage was between two people and it was not discouraged. However, in America laws forbade marriage between members of different ethnic groups. Amazingly if the contributors are called by a different group that the one that they represent that makes it fine. The world gets the benefit and no one is the wiser!

Laws were written in the judicial books that strictly prohibited marriage between Whites and Blacks. It was not until June 12, 1967 that the last laws against interracial marriages were struck down by the U.S. Supreme Court in <u>Loving vs. Commonwealth of Virginia</u>. The relationships between Whites and Blacks that culminate in marriage are still viewed as deviant behavior by many people in America today, both Blacks and Whites.

{According to Dr. Billingsley:

An ex-slave has told of getting married on one plantation: when you married, you have to jump over a broom three times. Dat was de license. If master seen two slaves together too much he would tell-em dye was married. Hit didn't make no difference if you wanted to or not, he would put you in de same cabin and make you live together, Marsa used to sometimes pick our wives fo' us. If he didn't have on his place enough women for the men, he would wait on de side of de road till a big wagon loaded with slaves come by. Den Marsa would stop de old nigger-trader and buy you a woman. Wasn't no use tryin' to pick one, 'cause Marsa wasn't gonna pay but so much for her. All he wanted was a young healthy one who looked like she could have children, whether she was purty or ugly as sin. }[14]

Marriages for Blacks was whatever the master said; if slaves spent any time together the maser would say that they were married, or the procedure of "jumping the broom" three times. But, that in itself would not keep the master from selling them apart. Slavery was based on an economic system.

When slavery finally ended, marriage licenses were in very high demand among Blacks. They wanted legal, officially licensed marriages; not the meaningless "jumping the broom" practice, that the planters would allow them in America. However, in certain tribes in Africa it was a part of the matrimonial ritual, and it was seen as an integral part of the entire ceremony. But the Jumping of the broom was a putdown compared to the legal "real marriage ceremony." Caucasians had legal marriages with papers, and licenses. Slaves could only jump the broom. It had no real meaning because anytime the master wanted a "wife of a slave, he just took her and lay with her; the woman was utterly defenseless. The male slave could not protect his woman or his bed. This is a prime example of how dehumanizing the state of slavery really was. Some modern Blacks will still "jump the broom" after the usual ceremony as a symbolic gesture to the past, and giving respect and honor to an African tradition. They usually hang the decorative broom on the family room wall to show it to all who visit the home.

> {Franklin & Moss stated:
> Few owners were sufficiently insensitive to human decency to admit that they were willing to divide slave families by sale. As a matter of fact, families were frequently advertised as being for sale together, but they were not always sold together. Slaves often brought higher prices when sold separately. The large numbers of single slaves on the market bears testimony to the rather ruthless separation of families that went on during the slave period. } [15]

Under slavery, some White men even sold their own bi-racial offspring in this trade of humans in order to gain economic wealth. However, marriages among slaves were not altogether absent in the United States, and were probably more common than most people recognized, although it was a much different institution with less structure; if the man decided not to remain in the marriage, there were no laws to compel him to stay with his family. Most families were torn apart anyway whenever a slave was needed on another plantation or if the owner needed additional money.

Finally, with the invention of the cotton gin, one would have thought this machine would drastically reduce the need for large numbers of slaves. However, just the opposite occurred when larger production plantations developed; this phenomenon made the need for slaves even greater. Slavery grew into a more lucrative business than ever before.

There was no need to treat slaves as humans, in fact, they became known as "beasts of burden." If a slave died, another was easily purchased, thus, slaves were seen as an inexhaustible resource. The myth soon spread among the Whites that Blacks had no "souls" and were, therefore, not human so it did not matter how cruelly they were treated. This carried over into religion, which meant that, even if a slave became a Christian, they would remain a slave.

With the notion that Blacks had no "souls," that meant Blacks did not have human qualities Whites were bound to respect. There was no limit to how long slaves could work in the fields. On the large plantations, masters continued working their slaves until they died from overwork; or were killed by the overseers. Whites took absolutely no responsibility for their behavior and they seemingly had no conscience about their treatment of Blacks at all. The taking of Africans was a "big economic business," as the economic wealth for the planters was built upon the backs of the slaves. Like their livestock, slaves were considered property, better known as chattel.

Very few Black men taught their children to fight back, even if it meant their deaths; the majority simply resigned themselves to just accept their fate. It seems, however, there were always people who would not accept conditions as they were, and tried to defend themselves. Europeans neglected to write about the many Africans who would rather die than become slaves. Many slaves died in transit over the Middle-passage, from jumping overboard, and starvation. Many slave uprisings were not written about for fear this type of rebellion would entice other slaves to rebel. Before slavery was over, slaves would often run away to try to find their loved ones. After slavery, it was a celebration to find their relatives who had been sold off; and to marry legally and put their families back together. Slaves were 'breed' like animals to produce more and more slaves.

Recent arguments denying slave breeding by some students of history cannot successfully refute these contemporary testimonies regarding the practice of slave breeding. Since the domestic slave trade and breeding were economic activities it is not surprising to find that; in the sale of slaves, there was the persistent practice of dividing families. Husbands were separated from their wives, and mothers were separated from their children. Some slaves were set free upon the death of their former masters.

Some masters when they were ready to die would issue what is known as a writ of Manumission to free certain slaves or all of their slaves upon their deaths. Some Blacks were also given a piece of land, and a little money to help give them a new start in life. The masters were subject to do t his especially if his offspring was involved.

This is not to say there was never any respect for basic human rights or ample sentimentality to prevent the separation of families. However, it would have been good business to keep more families together. The slaves would tend to be more content if there could have such a thing; having their families together would have been a plus for the plantation owners. Evidentially there were some old written laws in a few states which were not enforced regarding the selling of slave families. If they had been enforced; would have done much to ameliorate the conditions of slavery, but were almost wholly disregarded. Interestingly, the White man was the 'law' and whatever he did was not against the law. The laws were not meant for him to follow.

In many slave states, they didn't even have any such provisions of attempting to keep the slave families together. Children were sold as soon as they were weaned, others when they could walk, and still others when it was determined they could work (between 7-10 years old). This was a horrendous way to have to live; slavery was extremely harsh for millions of Black people. The fact that many survived slavery lends itself to the knowledge that determination and faith in God has its rewards. Not to mention the internal; and bodily strength and fortitude of slave ancestors that helped them to go through slavery so that their offspring could one day be free.

America owes a great debt to their darker brothers and sisters in America, for the many years of free labor it took to build this country into what it is today. Not many books give any credit to Blacks but they should. The apologies are fine, but the reparations would have been better. The Japanese in World War II were given some monetary benefits, but never the builders of this mighty nation of freedom and liberty! Somehow this does not seem to be fair or just.

Finally, after 400+ years in bondage, in January 1863, President Lincoln handed down the Emancipation Proclamation, which was implemented in only a few states at first, and finally enforced in 1865 for the remaining slave holding states. Blacks in America were finally "Free at Last"! This should have meant the beginning of a new life for former Black slaves. But there were some Whites with negative attitudes and actions that would stifle and hinder Blacks' and their attempts to achieve and to prosper here in the United States. Most of this was racial discrimination aimed at trying to keep Blacks from gainful employment, and housing.

Many of these unresolved problems for Black people still remain as many encounter negative behaviors on a daily basis in America. The practice of "Jim Crow" in the northern cities, along with discriminatory practices throughout the nation kept Black people in a lower socioeconomic level. Blacks have been free for 144 years, if one were to count from 1863 rather than (146) from 1865. However the vestiges of racism continue to haunt Blacks in America even into the 21st century!

Nothing shall be impossible unto you
-Matthew 17:20

Chapter VI.
While Moving Forward: The Black Family After Slavery (1865 to Present)

Ironically, the Emancipation Proclamation was a wonderful legal document that freed Blacks, but it neglected to provide them protection. Further, it seems this gesture was not necessarily for the benefit of Blacks.

According to Dr. Billingsley:

{"White institutions have been instituted for the advancement of Whites even when they have espoused causes that seemingly focus of the welfare of Blacks."} [1]

For example: (This author's note; President Lincoln wanted to "save the union;" even if it meant freeing of the slaves. However, slaves were not the President's primary focus; slaves would probably gain their freedom anyway as a result of the Civil War). [1]

In his startling conclusions regarding the crucial questions of freed slaves de Tocqueville continues along the same thought as Bennett.

{Alexis de Tocqueville stated, nearly 150 years ago:

"It was not for the good of the Negroes, but for that of the Whites, that measures are taken to abolish slavery in the United States." } [2]

As de Tocqueville stated, the abolishment of slavery was not in the interest of human rights, but for profit. It seems most things the White man does are in the interest of his wealth. It was a known fact that the division between the White Northerner and the White Southerner was based on money; slavery itself was an economic venture. However, whatever the real reason, slavery was finally ended, and Blacks were truly grateful.

Of course, freedom had advantages for the Black family; marriages among Blacks were legalized and recorded. Although family members could be whipped, run out of town, or murdered, they could not be sold away from their loved ones anymore. The period following emancipation was hard for the ex-slaves. They were homeless and did not know where their loved ones were; many starved to death. The government instituted the Freedmen's Bureau to help the newly freed Blacks, but this institution was short lived.

{According to Franklin and Moss:
Emancipation was, for some Negro slaves, a major life altering predicament for them…Reconstruction was a disastrous failure. However, there were 'windows of opportunity' that enabled a large number of families to survive; some managed to achieve stable forms of family life…. A few Negroes were able to achieve a high degree of social prominence….} [3]

A most interesting and poignant feature of the time were freed men searching for wives, children, and other family members who, years earlier, had been separated by sale or trade. While others after years of living together, many slaves with no marriage contracts looked for ministers to marry them legally. The U.S. Government did The Freedmen's Bureau to provide for the newly freed slaves.

Most freed men wanted to legally get married with a ring, and papers. Some families found their loved ones while others did not. However, their human spirit was unbroken and families grew stronger with every obstacle in their path.

The Freedmen's Bureau was established in the late 1860's for the newly freed slaves to offer them education, shelter, clothing and skills on doing for themselves. The bureau did not last long enough to really help the people become independent. This period was called Reconstruction. There was no more Master to answer questions or to provide some semblance of stabilization. Even though slavery was harsh, it was still harsher to have no place to live, no food, and not knowing what to do next. However, one of the first things that slaves did was to look for their loved ones who had been sold throughout the state to other plantations and/or out of the state. They had a sense of family and the meaning of being together with their loved ones.

This was a very dreary and sad time for this group of people. What should be done next? Some freed slaves had no choice but to return to the plantations of their former masters to work. The difference was now is that there would be supposedly some pay coming. This would help the Black families to buy seeds, and a few chickens to get started on becoming a self-sufficient people. However, Reconstruction ended too quickly and Blacks were forced to again seek work from former masters.

After the Reconstruction period ended, another form of servitude was put into place, sharecropping. This was just another disguise for slavery Blacks had endured for hundreds of years. The ex-slaves were kept on the old plantations and some were held there against their will. Again, they were told what to do and had to work for the former owners or be put in jail, or severely beaten. When the sharecroppers finished harvest, they had to wait until the plantation owners tallied up the procedures. Usually, Blacks were told there was no money for them, but they could have some of the harvest. No matter how much money the Black families made for the Whites, they ended up with nothing! And with the small amount of pay they had to again buy seeds for the next harvest. The cycle continued.

This sharecropping system continued until International Harvester made a cotton-picking machine, perfected in 1944, which replaced hundreds of Blacks. Now, Blacks did not have anything they could do and many left for the north. The "Great Migration" in America occurred between 1915 and 1945. Seemingly unbeknownst to the Whites, five million Blacks left the rural south for the "Promised Land" of the north.

When Blacks reached the northern cities, they were met with another limitation called Mr. "Jim Crow," the term given to discriminatory, racist attitudes of Whites in the north. Blacks were relegated to live in the worst parts of the cities and to work for low paying, menial jobs. To thousands of Blacks living in the north, this was freedom, and they would not trade it for the southern lifestyles they had left behind. The ugly head of racism was still doing its damage to deter and stop the progress of the Black family. Yet, Blacks were given rights by the Supreme Court when the laws of the various communities refused to follow them. This is what is known as de jure laws, but in fact they were not followed leading to the term defacto segregation meaning the way things really were in fact; Separate but Equal laws were never equal but always separate.

There is such an oxymoron when African Americans are treated so poorly, yet three of the Land Mark Decisions of the Supreme Court of America involved them. And the fourth involved a young Mexican man by the name of Miranda. This author will offer a brief synopsis of these cases. The Landmark years were: 1857, 1896, 1954, and 1966.

In 1857 there was a Supreme Court decision called The Dred Scott versus Stanford case. This decision involved a man named Dred Scott who had been a slave in the south, and when his master took him to the north, into a free state he wanted his freedom. But, the master refused to grant him his freedom. This case finally made it all the way to the Supreme Court where the Justices decided that there was nothing a Black could say or do that the White man was obliged to respect. In other words slavery was wherever the White man said it was!

{From Franklin & Moss:
From 1889 to 1922, 25 riots took place where 3,436 Black people were lynched or murdered. James Weldon Johnson called the summer of 1919 the "Red Summer," due to the high number of Blacks being killed. Many Black men, who had just returned from World War I and only wanted jobs, were lynched; still wearing the military uniforms they wore while defending their country. American diplomats did nothing to aid or protect them once they returned from the war. } 4

Some Whites did not want to see Blacks carry a weapon as it upset them. This was just another excuse to do harm to Blacks. These men had just returned from defending this country by upholding freedoms for others; and yet they were not free in their own country.

In 1896, the Supreme Court passed Plessy versus Ferguson. This law became known as the "Separate but Equal" clause which meant segregation was legal all over the United States. The pattern that was firmly established under slavery continued as "the way things were done." The entire nation knew the races were separate but never equal. No matter the difficult times, the Black family continued to thrive. This decision was based on Homer Plessy who was light skinned and had nice hair, he looked White however, the train driver knew his family and knew that he was a member of the Black group. When asked to sit at the back of the train car, Mr. Plessy replied, "I am as white as you are!" The Supreme Court decision decided that segregation was the right way for the "races" to coexist. This made it very difficult for Blacks to get ahead and to obtain a proper education.

However, the Black family was determined to survive, so all of the family members worked. Black women worked in White women's kitchens and cared for their children. While Black men, for the most part, worked at low-paying jobs that the White men no longer wanted to perform. With both parents working, the grandmother took over the care of the children; yet even with both parents working; they were barely able to feed their families. Segregation was still the law in the south and some of the north and; while this presented numerous problems for the Black family, it did not deter their determination to survive.

Emerging scholars of color could no longer ignore the Black family, as White scholars had previously done. With support from White institutions, these few Black scholars, and a handful of Whites, wrote about the Black family life. Many of these new-breed sociologists were concerned about the real problems facing the Black family. They concluded, after careful research, racism was the major contributing factor affecting the Black family.

Their contributions were factual and accurately written. The main writers of Black literature were historians and sociologists, many of whom came from Chicago universities. E. Franklin Frazier, a noted sociologist at the University of Chicago, wrote several books on the Black family. As Jesse Bernard and others often concluded information was most significant when written by an individual of the group being written about, this author agrees.

In the early 20th century Black households were intact with nuclear families; a father, mother, and children. The majority of babies born were into households with both parents. It is very important to note that the family is one of the most important Black institutions aside from the Church. Despite the numerous problems the Black family faced, it was determined to survive. Black men and women went into segregated units of the military by the hundreds.

{Some concepts were taken from Franklin and Moss:
Jobs, housing, and education were always problems for Negroes.
When Negro men returned for the military from World War I...
they were very disappointed, to have gone to war to protect

their country, and upon their arrival home, many were beaten and their guns taken away from them.... Also many could not find jobs even though they were trained for good jobs, the jobs were denied them, basically because of racism which tends to overt and directly affected one's life and livelihood. 5

Author's notes: {Most Blacks had little to no formal education other than what they might have received from the Military. These were very hard and discouraging periods in Black men's lives. }

In 1954 The Brown versus Board of Education was taken to the Supreme Court. This case involved a girl named Linda Brown; who was denied admittance to her local school because of her skin color. She had to be bused across town to a Black school. Her parents took the case to the Supreme Court. The decision was that segregation was inherently evil and wrong and therefore would be abolished. This was the beginning of the Civil Rights Laws that passed in 1964 and 1965. The Laws opened housing, the ability to eat in public restaurants, and to sit on various forms of transportation without having to always sit in the very back. Interestingly enough most young Blacks opt to sit in the very back when it was no longer mandatory. This author has never really understood this fact.

The fourth Land Mark decision involved a Mexican American, {Mr. Ernesto Miranda versus Arizona}. The Supreme Court decision was in 1966, Miranda was accused of raping a mildly retarded young woman. He was not given any rights at all: The right to remain silent, having a lawyer present, knowing that anything that you say or do can be held against you in a court of law). The things that happened to Mr. Miranda happened on a regular basis to other Black youth and Latino youth; thanks to him the laws even though stringent when it came to dealing with minorities had to acknowledge their rights. Presently, there are many Blacks in prison after being denied their rights and nothing was done about it. There are agencies today that are trying to free the men that have been falsely imprisoned.

The Black families' stability increased until the number of new births among Blacks began to decline in the 1960s. After this period, many couples opted not to have children or, only one or two. This was due to the economics involved with caring for a large family in uncertain financial times. However these families were intact with a mother and a father.

This decline continues today, even considering the high numbers of un-wed teen-age mothers within the Black population. One factor contributing to this decline is the unavailability of marriage-aged Black males due to incarceration, homosexuality, and interracial marriages. Other factors include a high infant mortality rate, increased number of abortions, and utilizing contraceptives. Unfortunately, single motherhood has also become a cultural norm. Which is seen as a negative in America, most other groups still adhere to a nuclear family. With the proper examples and instruction this too can be turned around for the betterment of the group.

At the time, many books about Blacks were being written which established a self-fulfilling prophecy. American society believed what was written in these books; as did the news media and, interestingly enough, so did many Blacks. Please note: These are a "beaten" people who, through the many years of maltreatment, have internalized negatives about themselves and their self-worth. After hundreds of years, it was very difficult to change this self-perception in just a few generations; yet, change has begun to "blossom" throughout the Black communities throughout America.

Black parents have always wanted their children to have a better life then they did. Previously, most Black youth were properly dressed and lived in well-maintained homes or apartments; cleanliness was demanded. These children were taught morality, manners, and to take pride in their appearance. Somehow, some of these fundamentals seem to have been lost in recent years. The damage to the Black group has come not only from the past physical abuse but also from the mental abuse. Mental abuse or psychological abuse takes many years and sometime it may never completely dissipate.

For example, in slavery, the Black man was emasculated and trained, not only physically but also psychologically, to "protect White people;" and not to care about his own people. This psychological damage was most severe when internalized and passed on to future generations. Black slave men were also used to sire children for trade, creating a disconnection with the role of parenting. Regrettably, this trend seemingly has also carried over into the present times. Once freed, the institution perpetuated this emasculation by denying Black men decent jobs, housing, and other means of supporting their families. Thus, producing the broken Black family without the man figure that many sociologists have written about.

In contrast, an important role among Blacks during slavery (that has all but vanished) was the role of the granny, "the guardian of the generations." (Frazier, 1963) The position of the oldest woman in a family was, traditionally, an extremely important one as the matriarch. The grandmother played an important part even under slavery, and was "highly esteemed by both the slaves and the masters." She was wisdom personified and the keeper of the family history, to be passed on to future generations. In the master's house, she was very often called "mammy" or "granny" whose history and tradition have been idealized because of her loyalty and affection. Because of her intimate relations with the Whites "all family secrets," as Calhoun observes, were in her keeping as the defender of the family honor. The ties of affection between her and her charges were never outgrown.

Often, she was the confidential advisor of the older members of the household; to young mothers, she was an authority on first babies. The Black granny was a true matriarch; a profoundly powerful and stabilizing female head of family. Even today, film and media often contain the images of strong black women in roles of "big mama" or the granny. In modern times the most successful youth are reared in a home with a grandmother living with them or one that lives nearby. Most parents have to work to survive and the grandmother is the one with her wisdom rearing the children. My heart-felt thanks to my grandmother and to all the grandmothers of the world who help to instill positive and helpful methods to children to help them to make the better choices in life. However, in some homes the Black woman has had to be the mother and the father for her children.

More recently, the Black woman has had to assume some roles assigned for males, especially when it comes to employment, primarily because of racism that hindered him. In a planned attempt to keep the Black man in a subservient role. Therefore, many of the family duties have fallen upon the woman to fulfill. This trend has, unfortunately, been pervasive and problematic for the Black family. But, there are some Black men that refuse to get an education and also refuse to work; Author's notes: {The slave mentality is still operative today in many communities.} These are called "professional baby-makers," they hop from bed- to -bed making babies but not caring for any of them. This has got to stop as there are far too many children growing up without positive father figures in their lives. This author's note: There is an incredible need in Black communities for positive role models they can either be Black or White a positive man is needed no matter the ethnic origin. Author's note: My son Marcos had a positive White role model, and today my son is an Electrical Engineer.

Parents need to teach their boys it is wrong to impregnate a girl and then "leave her holding the bag." Parents further need to teach their young girls that "saving oneself" for marriage is a wonderful thing to do. Boys do not "love you /they lust" after you that is the real four letter word for the "I love you baby." Churches have abdicated their burden to teach and train the young. Churches should also have more groups geared toward young people helping them to live in this today environment along with biblical teachings.

Providing for the family was a role left to the Black women inherited from slavery because, at any time, the master could decide to sell the man off to another plantation. And often the master "would sire" the Black males out to insure his slave population would continue to grow and the man had no responsibility for their children. Would it be possible for someone to inform young Black men that slavery is over! If the family was to survive, it had to depend upon the woman, who had to be strong and stable. These traits have somehow been seen as negative, rather than positive, traits. Usually, there was always a granny around to share her wisdom with the mother.

Black women were the stable force in the Black family down through the generations. The Black woman has had to be strong and willing to keep the family together in spite of the formidable circumstances in which she found herself. There was a conspiracy of sorts against the Black man; he was always being called "boy" and then, when he was old enough, when his hair had turned gray, he was called "uncle." These insulting names only tended to diminish the Black males' status in his family and in the work force.

With ineffective weapons, the Black male had to wage a constant battle against an arsenal of barriers. Education and training are much-needed devices in this conflict, yet they alone do not make the man. The Black man must draw on his personal strength and fortitude to sustain himself and his family against the odds.

Researchers have speculated that the female oriented household has contributed to the emasculation of the Black male. However, there is usually a grandfather, a boyfriend, a male teacher or a scout leader who demonstrates the characteristics of male role models. Some Black men have adopted a "Black" way of walking, talking, dressing, and even acting, to support the position that they are men; in every aspect of the word.

There has always tended to be the Black male that was belligerent, rude, arrogant, and hostile in his dealings with women either Black or White. These "bad Blacks" were usually known in various neighborhoods and most people avoided them. Then, there is the professional Black male that is highly educated and has successfully navigated the waters leading to wealth, position and some status. Attempting to reach out and help others will not damage the struggle made to 'arrive.' Sometimes a professional Black male will help a member or two of his family to obtain success, or will at least buy their mothers a house. Some will even start funds for minority children, but most marry White and forget that they are still Black no matter the temporary status of being successful in the White man's world. Usually, even with some of the trappings of success there is always the threat that one could lose everything if one attempted to make waves or become known as a "trouble maker." In other words the need to share the wealth has not been a reality in most Black areas.

The many famous athletics, singers, and actors/actresses some have make great strides to reach out to other less fortunate Blacks. Among the known contributors are Oprah Winfrey and Dr. Bill Cosby. Some famous Blacks have simply claimed the fame and moved on with their own lives without regard for anyone else. In recent years many professional Blacks have 'stepped up to the plate' and began to give back to their communities throughout the nation. The fact is that none of the privileges that are taken for granted would have been possible without the sacrifices of Blacks marching, protesting, and struggling for some semblance of equality; as my mother Ella would always say 'down through the years.' The Black group had many "bridge builders" to be eternally grateful to; among those were Banneker, Carver, Marshall, and Dr. King.

Dr. Martin Luther King, Jr. comes to mind as a hero of great proportions and his undying struggle to help free the masses of down trodden; and unequally treated Blacks. He was also concerned with others and the poor no matter which group they belonged. Thanks to his efforts along with others' there are many opportunities available today than ever before for most Americans. The struggle continues because the "root" problems have not been thoroughly eradicated from America.

In the 1960s, a "new" student emerged in American society who wanted to know more. He/she raised questions concerning Blacks and the inadequately explained answers that Whites were writing. This was a time when Blacks were "Black and Proud, "and they wanted to find their "roots." Alex Haley did much to contribute to the flood of new materials on the market on Blacks from a Black perspective. (Author's note: Just a few years before this time, it would be "fighting words" if a Black person was called "Black)." It seemed that when James Brown sung out "I'm Black and I'm proud!" It was also stated that there was a "new Black" alive in America, that would not be content to exist under segregation and all that 'evil' entailed.

There was a new change that arrived in the Black communities throughout America; now most Blacks were proud of their heritage, and their looks. Some merchants in White America were not happy; they were losing money on hair straightening products, clothes, shoes and pursuing that "Barbie" look. Black women dressed similar, and had their hair styled to be straight. Some Whites found this new phenomenon to be very disturbing. Blacks were wearing their hair "natural," "Afros" and African type clothing now. Everything was done to regain an African History that was once seen as "negative;" it was now being thought of as positive. Some writers and newspersons were asking questions of Blacks attempting to find out what was going on. This was amazing and unsettling to many in White America. Some of the questions being asked were "what do you people want?" (Note: Quite a few stores were losing money as a result of this new trend. Now African Americans were opening their own stores and providing the African clothes many times directly from African merchants).

Some writers focused upon poverty; the more they investigated the more they found that Blacks were over-represented as being poor; especially since their numbers make up a smaller percentage of the population in America according to the Census Bureau. This is also true of the prison scenario. Black males make up over 60 percent of all the persons imprisoned, and yet we are told Blacks make up only about 13 percent of the total population here in America. One can quickly assume that something is not quite right with our judicial system. These poverty experts soon found that there was a connection between poverty and the Black family. (Author's note: If the statistics were correct then the majority of people on the welfare rolls had to be White, as they were reported to have been the majority in America). When this fact was finally fathomed out; less was said about people being on welfare. Welfare was news, when Blacks were suspected as being the largest users of the system. The Black family has always important to Blacks in America.

The extended family was an important aspect of the Black family, which included the grandparents, cousins, aunts, or uncles. In other words, there was always someone there to help with the children, and to teach them morals and values. The extended family concept came from Africa. The notion that other family members would live in one house and share the rearing of the children, keeping traditions and values instilled in the youth. This practice, however, was very foreign to Whites in America; of course, it was viewed as "deviant behavior." Any behavior or patterns not from Europe was seen as outside the "norm." Therefore, it should be studied and researched. The Black family stayed under the microscope for many years.

In 1965, Daniel P. Moynihan wrote a devastating book, *The Pathology of the Negro Family*. The basic premise was that the Black family was pathological in nature endemic to Blacks. Now the Black family was "put under the microscope and was being dissected in the media. A large focus seemed to be on the female head of household and babies being born without fathers in the home. The 1960's census single parent chart was high for Black females as well as for White females. There was no mention however of the 75% intact (both parents in the home) Black families in America. This report, unfortunately, became a "self-fulfilling prophecy." Moynihan and other sociologists at the time saw the Black family as being deviant from the White family structure.

This report further stated the high poverty levels among Black single females. All Black people faced poverty, prejudice, and historical subjugation because of their skin color. The fact is true because they are Black and live in a racist society. Sociologists called the "poor" women's plight "the feminization of poverty." This held doubly true for the Black mothers in America. Many studies have been done concerning this sociological phenomenon in a country where racism is "as American as apple pie."

When Whites are in the poverty levels, they only face poverty; not both poverty and color. Black women have traditionally been the "mainstay," if you will, for the Black family; the major reason being that racism has been perpetrated against the Black male.

In 1964 and '65, when the Civil Rights laws were passed, the Separate but Equal doctrine was dismantled. However, many aspects of racism still persist; in more subtle covert ways and sometimes in overt ways.

There is still a wide disparity between the education of Black youth and White youth in this country. There are vast differences in test scores; in many schools in America. Why? The bottom line is still associated with various forms of racism. The more blatant forms of brutality came in the form of "open season for killing Black males" in the not so distant past.

Examples would be the Rodney King beating, and the police killings of young Black males throughout the nation. In fact Black youth were targeted to the extent that Black authors began writing about the possible extinction of Black males in America. For many months newspaper headlines were about how the police shot a Black youth (always in self-defense according to the officer that did the shooting). The police were acquitted even when the victim was shot in the back; or shot without carrying a weapon, even though the police said that the victim threatened them with a weapon.

Black men became increasingly discouraged with the continuous discrimination and oppression that plagued their existence on every level. The Black family as a unit began to crumble. The Black woman was left with the responsibilities of financially, mentally, and physically supporting the family. This time period witnessed a rise in criminal behavior, which led to the incarceration of numerous Black men. This further compounded the problems that the Black family was and is still experiencing.

Throughout the many years of racial discrimination, oppression, and degradation caused many Black people to lose hope, faith in God, the church, and themselves. Too many Black families today are headed by single women and by children who are bearing children at a time when they are incapable of caring for themselves. At the same time, Black boys have become discouraged and have resorted to the so-called "gangster lifestyle" of drugs, sex, and violence. "Rap" music with its vile lyrics consisting mostly of put downs against Black women. Which are negative and a distortion of women of color. There were and are still periods of "drive-by shootings," in many areas in the minority sections in America. Black-on-Black crime was the headlines on a regular basis. This devastating situation of Black-on- Black crime has almost claimed an entire generation of Black children. Alcohol and other "hard" drugs permeate the Black community seemingly, with the blessings, or so it seems, of the legal system. Nothing much is done when the illegal drugs are in the minority neighborhoods, it takes another stance when these illegal drugs include "White children." Again this is an example of "the chains on the mind" mentality. Hatred of oneself and others that look the same has been the main reason for Black on Black crimes.

Where do these drugs come from? Are Blacks flying planes from one country to another to pick up the drugs? (This author does not think so). These drugs are a large part of our American economy (the underground society). If the American Government wanted to halt drugs, it would be stopped today. Illegal drugs, like all other businesses in American society, have placed in these United States, or so it seems. The illegal drugs are brought into America by plane, boats, and by smuggling it into the country. Most drugs are brought by the wealthy and persons with the ability to rent or own the mechanisms to bring in the contraband. However, it ends up on the streets of the ghettos and the barrios throughout the nation. These poor hustlers are being jailed and sent to prison by the hundreds; they are the "small fish." Very seldom do the persons at the top get caught, which is very unfair and the punishment works against the "penny anti" street thugs. The real perpetrators are still in the illegal drug business. And the "top men" (drug pushers) are very wealthy and living in upper neighborhoods throughout America.

Since the 1980s, and up to the present day, there have been many interracial marriages. These marriages have produced "so-called" bi-racial offspring; they make up a large segment of the total American population. This adds to the total number of Blacks not including the many thousands of "mulattos" that were born throughout slavery, and after, some of which are passing for White. If the truth were told, the majority in America would be Blacks or African Americans, because slavery produced many mulattoes (some so fair that they married and lived their lives in a white world.) Negating any contact with their Black family members, what a huge burden to carry throughout one's life. (In this author's opinion my family would always come first. If I am loved then my background or ethnicity should not matter). Love is supposedly blind, and it is in the eye of the beholder~ well, maybe not.

One of the ways to tell if a Black is "passing" is that most of them will not have any children, or will say that they are unable to bear children. Therefore, these families opt for adoption. This, of course, means that they usually adopt a "white" child or two and now their family is complete. The Black partner is always afraid of being 'caught.' There is very little chance they will try to have their own children, because of them might come out 'brown.' To live in this 'white world' means the total denial of their family ties, what a burden to carry throughout ones life. (Author's note: Please know that in America if one has a "drop" of Black blood he/she could be considered Black). There are however, some very beautiful mixed blue-eyed, blonde children who will one day have to choose their ethnic heritage, if America continues to "label" its citizens. I understand in recent years the mother has the duty to label her child whatever she considers the child to be. Why the need to be identified with one group or the other seems nonsensical to this author. America does not need its labels or boxes; in the twenty-first century there should not be any need for them.

Some Whites some years ago came up with more terminology and concepts including "let's allow Blacks to assimilate," by "melting" into White society which has not been completely possible. Assimilation then became pluralism (allowing members of other groups to enjoy and retain their culture while working and performing in the wider society). Today, the term is the "salad bowl," with diversity and multiculturalism, where all groups are to be celebrated and validated. It is unfortunate that America has to label all groups; and to consider color first in America! (Note: This author visited Paris, France and was greeted at the airport as an "American)."

The destiny of all Black people is invariably connected to the future of the Black family. Black marriages need to be stable and to remain for the sake of the children. The out of wedlock practices by youth needs to stop; the youth need to consider marriage first and children second. The Black community, in order to survive, needs to start their own economic institutions, as they have had in the past. The Black community of years past gave Blacks a real sense of community. These institutions enriched; and served in many functions that traditionally belonged to the Black communities of old. Integration is fine, but it has not totally worked for all Blacks in America. And it has not been the "ticket out" that some Blacks had hoped for.

A few Black women have found it difficult to find a "good" Black man, some have opted to become impregnated by artificial insemination or have resigned to the idea of just being in a relationship sans marriage. Many of these Black women who have made these choices are professional, middle-class women, with financial security who want children. Adoption is not an option for those who want their own children. Some Black women are also moving toward the women's liberation movement (or feminism—a movement in conjunction with White women to a certain extent). Still others are going back to the submissive, supportive roles held by Black women in years past. While more progressive Black "Sisters" have picked up some of the ways of African women to bring in some cultural elements to their families; for example Kwanzaa celebrations. However, the "old" role of the past, which included being submissive, was not a "reality" in her life.

Why can't a Black woman find a 'good Black man?' Here are seven reasons:

- Incarcerated in either jail/prison
- Married outside of their own group
- Homosexual/gay
- Die young/drive by shootings/gang related
- Shortage of male babies
- Insufficient education/skills
- Married within the group

Today in 2009, Black females are the heads of their households in greater numbers than comparative groups. More than ever, the extended family kinship system is needed within the African American communities. It was once seen as dysfunctional to have other members in a household, but for the Black family it was always functional and needed.

{According to Moyd:
The next problem that affects the Black family is the welfare system. A percentage of Blacks, namely women who are single, divorced, or widowed with a child and without a male presence in the home rely on welfare for economic survival. The funny thing is males were not allowed to be part of a family if it was to receive welfare (sounds like another case of "slavery" time practices). Because of this prerequisite, many times Black men were

forced to leave their families during hard economic terms in order that his family could eat and survive.} [6]

(Author's note: I believe that women should work if physically and mentally possible). (However, Welfare in this author's opinion was just another form of slavery. Someone is always directing and knowing every aspect of a woman's life, which is too much "control" to live under). The best alternative would be to get an education and then a job. Many times Black men could not get a job that would pay enough to take care of a family. Some of the lack of employment was a direct way to keep the Black man subject to the role of "boy."

Some of these concerned men made arrangements to camp with their peers by day and sleep with their families by night. Sadly, this simple survival technique did not last long. When the welfare agent found out, a cadre of night agents was organized, whose only function was to spy out and to raid these Black homes (criminally breaking in if necessary) and catch these fathers sleeping with their families. This was the old way and has been continued until recent years. How horrible, even when families tried to stay together it was not possible.

The newspapers headlines would state 'Black Father Goes to Jail for Welfare Cheating' reporting the results of these raids in both Black and White newspapers…However, this was simply another ploy to disrupt the Black family, if the male could not find work, then he could not take care of his family. (Author's note: The real truth is that the majority of people on welfare are White, not Black).

While the majority of Black fathers care for their children, some are unable to do very much because of low-paying jobs, but they did/do what they could/can. However, since the institution of marriage has been abandoned for several decades, the Black women are virtually "without a man" today. Some Black men seem to be playing out some outdated parts that are reminiscent of slavery. In other words, father the child, but you do not have any responsibility for its care. The state will supplement the mother and take care of your charges. This is not a positive mind-set, and it has permeated a void in the Black family especially for the male child. Good fatherly role models are very hard to find anymore for many Black families.

This practice of not taking responsibility must stop; young people must become educated, and self-sufficient. These chains of the past must be shed, and a new approach to life in America must spring forth. Black men, looking for jobs that provide substantial, compensation usually requires at least a high school education if not a college education. High school diplomas are not enough. For many years, higher education was not available for Blacks, especially males. Even today, racism keeps many qualified Black men from employment and higher education. However, this was not the case for most Black women in America, especially in recent years. More Black women are highly educated and have meaningful positions in corporate offices throughout America. Today the bondage is not the "chains" on the body, but the chains are on the minds. This is a more difficult "chain" to break, and many of Willie Lynches' predictions unfortunately have held true within the Black community to this present day!

However, racism has again reared its "ugly head," there was a recent incident in Jena, Louisiana. A group of boys White and Black engaged in an altercation in 2006. The Whites had hung "nooses" on a tree called "The White Tree." Some Blacks sat under the tree, and the scuffle began. However, the White students were given a lenient sentence and the six Blacks were ordered to a harsher sentence totaling a 100 years in prison. The Black students were tried as adults. Does this sound like 21st Century America? In 2007, only after the news media gave some attention to this matter were the six Black youth released from prison. In America there is always a call for the "world" to become Democratic, and fair. Somehow this does not seem to be the way it really is in America. This author: Finds it highly hypocritical of America to demand humane treatment of other countries citizens and not 'clean up America' first then help the world!

How dare America "preach" to the rest of the world when America does not guarantee equality to all of its citizens. Blacks have come a long way; but unfortunately it seems they still have more to over-come. America, while attempting to finally over-come "race" problems in America, is deficient as the struggle continues. (Note: This author thinks that there is only one race and that is the "human" race). We are all a part of the human family called Homo- Sapiens. There is no sub-variety of humans. If labels were necessary then "ethnicity" would seem to be a more realistic term; than"race."

More and more, Black men are not around long enough to build a marriage or a strong relationship with Black women. The biggest culprit of this crime is a society that has locked the Black male out of the mainstream through a pattern of bias actions. This is seemingly a "throwback" to slavery, where the males were to "sire" children and the master would then sell them for a profit. There was no connection then and it seems for whatever reasons there are not many connec-tions today in far too many cases. A Black male cannot commit to a family when he has no job or no chances of getting one either because of a prior record (jail or prison). For many African American men, there has not been much hope of being completely successful; this situation seemed to be by design. The new migration seems to have escaped the attention of the masses, when thousands of Blacks moved north to large cities for work.

The "Great Migration" of the 1940's went virtually unnoticed by the majority group. This caused an explosion of mechanized or indus-trial revolution in the south. Black male power was largely missing in the south; there were only a few older men and boys to work left at home with the mother and or the grandmother. When a job was se-cured by the husband he would send for the rest of the family and they too would move north. The north had its share of problems how-ever with something called "Jim Crow." These were restrictive laws that were meant to keep Blacks in their place. This included housing, jobs, and low salaries. Blacks faced a new set of obstacles in the north they were not as blatant as they had been in the south. Black men were finally able to work, and began to care for their families. Various com-munities were formed as each ethnic group joined together to help one another. These little ethnic communities were known for a specialty; i.e. food, clothing, or jewelry. This came very close to pluralism in its best form. Some of these group members worked outside their community yet, they spent their money and their time within their specified communities.

Before integration, Black professional people who had worked very hard and received an extensive education headed most of the Black families. These Black families served as examples to other Black families in the communities throughout the nation to inspire them. Many families strived to achieve the American dream. Most of these positive examples were lost in the integration process because these people moved from the old neighborhoods and lost the sense of community. It was vital during segregation for Blacks to own their own businesses and to have their own professional providers. These people were the "role-models;" Blacks depended upon themselves, not outsiders. Black people were achievers and hard workers; some of that seems to have been lost, in recent years.

Blacks contributed greatly to America and the world all Americans should be thankful for them. However, the inter-relationships between Black men and women have seemingly changed in that past thirty years. The strong family bonds that once existed, now seems to be on the decline. The search for wealth and riches has caused many Black people to lose their perspective on the value of life and the importance of raising a productive family. Fortunately, this has only been a small fraction of the African American or Black group. However, the majority of Black families seem to believe the notion that their children; will achieve much more than they were able to. Each generation tends to hope for a better tomorrow for their children. The positive changes must come and come soon.

The time for change is now. For a people to survive there needs to be fluid dynamic change, as nothing ever remains static. We live in an ever-changing world. If the Black family is to survive, then it is vital to move toward positive methods to keep the family unit intact. Black families constitute an important segment of social life in America.

{According to Macionis.
In the 1996, the Black families made up 46 percent, female-headed families 47 percent and male-headed families made up 7%. In 1996 the typical African American family earned $26,522, only 63% of the national standard. People of African ancestry are also three times as likely as whites to be poor, and poverty means that families experience unemployment, underemployment, and, in some cases, a physical environment replete with crime and drug abuse. } 7

This was and is a serious obstacle especially for Black families. They need fathers to provide model positive behavior. Meaning simply, that the man needs to be the "head" of the household, he needs to work, and to provide for his family. He should be tender and loving to his wife and children. These examples will show the young boys how a "real" man behaves and provides for his family.

However, the significance of Black families lies not in numbers, but in the crucial role Blacks have played in the evolution of World History and in American society. This happened, in spite of the problems that Blacks have been struggling under. Therefore, with a concerted effort to solidify and strengthen the family; Blacks would have much more to offer their communities and the broader society.

Blacks will need to pick up the mantle and meet the challenge; by writing, researching, and studying to have their proper place in American history. In recent years, there have been positive studies written by Blacks and others with a realistic and sincere effort, to counteract the negative images that have been written from the past.

The Black family has sustained itself throughout the horrors of slavery and Reconstruction; the early 1900s, down through the years until this present year, 2009. It is hoped and prayed that the Black family will remain a viable force in the lives of African Americans. The family and the Church are all that the African Americans could hold on to in America. These two institutions are major segments of sociological theory and practice. And, these two institutions must be preserved if the Black group is to survive with dignity and a true sense of "pride" as they march proudly further into the 21st century!

"In the World ye shall have Tribulations: but be of good cheer; I have overcome the world."
-John 16:33

Chapter VII.
The Black Church/Religion

African American religion did just come about when Africans were reintroduced to the New World. Christianity began in the area surrounding Africa. According to the Original African Heritage Study Bible, Ethiopia was the first Christian nation. Africans did not need Europeans to save their "souls." Africans were the original people and they knew God. However, through the period of hundreds of years, some Africans began to worship other gods and they lost the original zest for the omnipresent God. This is similar to what happened to the children of Israel (the Jewish nation), they turned away from God. As an example, they struggled in slavery under the Egyptian Pharaoh for four hundred and thirty-two years; Africans in America suffered for nearly the same period of years under European dominance. Both groups suffered similar fates for their disobedience to God. God is no respecter of humankind. Ethiopia is mentioned in the Holy Bible over forty times and Egypt is mentioned over one hundred times.

(It seems to this author that Africa was a very important place to God).

During slavery in America, Blacks were forced to attend church with their slave owners so they had to sneak around at night to practice their own religious beliefs. Throughout slavery there were a group of Blacks that would meet usually by the riverside to worship God. In order to better understand the Black religion in America, we now have scholars to provide better research into the past attempting to understand what Black people believed from ancient times to the present.

Most of the ensuing information will come directly from the <u>Original African</u>
<u>Heritage Study Bible:</u>

Christianity originated in Africa because God gave His creation His words and laws. Christians are of the group of God. This was prior to the birth of Jesus, His son, of whom Christianity was officially named many thousands of years later. The people were first called Christians in a city called Bethel, because they were followers of Christ.

{Also in Psalm 68:31:

Princes shall come out of Egypt; Ethiopia shall soon stretch out her hands unto God.} [1]

(Author's note: This reminds this author of when God sent Joseph, and Mary and Jesus to Egypt because King Herod wanted the child killed. Think for a moment if they looked like Europeans how could they possibly hide in Black Egypt? Europeans have been writing about how Egypt is a part of the Middle East or a part of southern Europe; it is not true; Egypt is still northern Africa)!

{According to the Original African Heritage Study Bible: "The Ancient Black Christians"
John Mark took his teachings of Christ into Egypt, but the original Christianity was already there. Keep in mind that the Garden of Eden was located in the Eastern section of Africa where the Tigris and Euphrates rivers intersect. John Mark was ordained the first bishop of Africa. By the year 189 A.D., Christianity appears to have been well established all across North Africa. Many Christians died in the persecution directed against them by other religious zealots like the Romans and Muslims. There were many religious wars and persecutions in history and yet Africa is mentioned in very few texts. } [2]

Africa was a Christian nation as God was the Father of Adam and Eve. The Bible has many things that need to be explored, and understood.

{St. Maurice was a Black general in 287 A.D. He and his men became Christians while stationed in Africa. They were fervent believers in God, and would not serve the pagan gods anymore. After his death in Europe, St. Maurice became highly revered in the Christian arena.} [3]

St Maurice was a revered statue in the Catholic faith. Africa had many early Christians.

{Finally, the edict of Milan, in about 300 A.D., was issued by the Roman state, granting social and political freedom to Christians. It was no longer a crime to practice the Christian faith.} [4]

Surprisingly enough, Catholics were not considered to be Christian by most of the North African and Ethiopian congregations at this time in history. But then again, most of the Catholic "religious" holidays are also based upon holidays of "pagan" people; now converted Christians. Today, Christians practice these holidays out of tradition; recognized by the Catholic Church; among those are Halloween, Easter, and Christmas. Most knowledgeable Christians realize this truth, and have attached a religious meaning for these holidays; therefore, aligning themselves with Catholic practices and belief systems. The exception is Halloween, which, for the most part, Protestants have left for Catholics to celebrate.

Due to the edict of Milan, Christianity was now free to prosper and develop. The history of the African involvement in the early church continues with many sagas and contributions made by Africans. It has been repeatedly stated that Christianity began in Africa, which was widespread prior to the European Christian era. By the beginning of the 4th century, in Eastern Africa, Christianity became the state religion of Ethiopia. In Roman Africa, St. Augustine had succeeded in spreading his Christian influence early in the 5th century, and also to the known world at this time.

Soon after, the Nubians of the Middle Nile and some of their neighbors to the south embraced the Christian faith. Although it seemed that most of Africa had accepted and embraced this religion, there were vast areas in the Americas that did not want to deal with the Christian faith. They held on to their indigenous faiths. Similarly, the version of Christianity that was made popular in Europe, never achieved full dominance in Africa.

Africans did not wait for either the Muslims or the European Christians to provide a religious basis for their existence. For many centuries, Blacks had relied on their own special brand of theology and spirituality to explain the mysteries of the universe and their destiny as human beings. But, they always knew God, as they conceived of Him, even if some tribes/clans had several beliefs in lesser gods. Almost everywhere, there was the belief that the great men of the past, or the "founding ancestors," had much to do with the present and the future of the Black Americans' worship practices.

{John G. Jackson's stated: Man, God, & Civilization
The barbarians began to overrun the Western Roman Empire in the early part of the fifth century, and by the end of that century Roman civilization was in ruins. Europe then entered upon the long night of the Dark Ages, which lasted for five hundred years (500-1100 A.D). The Dark Ages, as Professor Thompson said truly, "Were at least as much due to the corruption of the Church as to the decay of Roman civilization or…barbarian invasions." It was at this period in history that chronicled many horrors; it was the beginning of Europe's conversion to Christianity. "Could the full history of the conversion of Europe to Christianity be written," said Dr. Briffault, "it would present a tale of horror more appalling than that of the Christianity of Spain by the Inquisition.} [5]

The Christian religion had been imposed upon the people of Europe in much the same manner as it was imposed on Mexico and Peru, in the course of whose conversions continues.

{According to the Original African Heritage Study Bible:

…. De Las Casas estimates that twelve million died as most were butchered, tortured and burnt alive. De Casas was the head Priest of the Catholic Church who gave the orders to take Africans into slavery in order to spare the Native Americans, or "Indians," in America. Some so-called "Christians" were the major perpetrators of the enslavement of Africans and other people of color throughout the world.} [6]

It seems that the Church will have much to answer to God concerning the treatment rather mistreatment of humans in this world.

{Rogers's wrote the use of Negroes came about thusly:
Good Bishop Las Casas (1474-1566) seeing the Indians dying under the tasks imposed on them suggested the use of Africans instead-a step that has left a negative legacy for Las Casas is known in history as" the father of the African slave trade." He lived to regret it bitterly. He said in his old age that had he known its consequences, "he wouldn't have done it for the world."} [7]

This means that no matter the station in life a man of the cloth can conceivably do hateful and barbaric things to others all in the name of God. If the church went along with slavery so did the average White man it was about finances. Slavery was an economic venture for the European. The church not only perpetuated slavery, but also created it where it had never existed under Roman law.

Author's notes: No one could honestly say that America would not be the grand country that it is if it had not been for the African slave that built this country from nothing, {by their blood, sweat and tears}. Blacks were artisans, and skilled ironworkers. In fact on the top of the Capitol in Washington, D.C., is the Statue of freedom. A Negro slave erected the statue and placed into position his name was Phillip Reed. Have you ever heard this fact before?

> {Rogers's continues:
> Planters would say, "Negroes are the lifeblood of the plantations. Without them we could not exist." Southern planters, quoting the Bible, called Africans "the one thing needful."...."Everything is by God's blessing in good condition and in consequence of the employment of Negro slaves." }[8]

This statement was from a man of the cloth, no wonder in modern times some African Americans thought that Christianity was not for persons of color. This is an example of how slaves were thought of and were often referred to as a blessing from God. In other words, God knew, and was in agreement that Africans needed to be enslaved by the Europeans at that time.

Blacks participated in many historic events, especially all of the Wars starting with the Revolutionary War. However, the history books will not reveal these truths, as they have been virtually thrown out, and/or left out of the historical pages deliberately. If they are mentioned it is relegated to a sentence or two.

> {Rogers's wrote concerning Patrick Henry stated:
> He deplored "the necessity of holding his fellow-men in bondage." But that "their manumission is incompatible with the felicity of the country." Thomas Jefferson and a few other so-called humane slave owners said the same thing.} [9]

It is fine to feel compassion but without the power to legislate changes in the law was not very reassuring. The enslaved were needed to keep the plantation owners wealthy and prosperous. Thomas Jefferson owned slaves it was said that he treated them humanely he should after all he had several children by Sally Hemmings a Black female slave. Years ago the Jefferson's had a 'family reunion and all of them attended the White side and the Black side. Paul wrote of a slave in the Bible.

St. Paul advised one slave, Onesimus, in the Holy Bible to return to his master and counseled slaves to be obedient to their owners, again this was because of the feelings that slaves were persons of worth and were not all to be treated poorly in this case Paul knew Philemon, and had converted him to become a Christian. Paul's relation with Philemon led him to believe that Onesimus was no longer considered a slave but now a brother as they were both Christians. This was a time the love of God was in the hearts of both master and slave, thereby providing for a better working relationship. Rather a brotherhood type relationship.

As this author has stated American slavery was one of the worst and harshest and brutal in recorded history after the so-called enlighten period of history. In the ancient period in history, slavery was the "norm." It was a way of life from biblical times throughout the 18th century. Mankind seems to have forgotten that all men had a "common" beginning.

All people were from the one common human family (Adam and Eve) God orchestrated creation. We must remember that when God stopped the people from the building of the Tower of Babel, He spread them to the four corners of the earth and confused their language. At that time prior to God stepping in the people all spoke one common language and they lived together. However, after the separation of the people there was no more harmony or getting along.

Blacks were determined to achieve no matter that circumstances. These Churches grew and most are still active today.

{Daniel P. Seaton states from the Original African Heritage Study Bible:
Because these Hamites were an important people, attempts have been made o rob them of their proper place in the catalogue of the races. The Bible tells us plainly that the Phoenicians were descendants of Canaan, the son of Ham, and anyone who will take the time to read the Bible account of their lineage must concede the fact.} [10]

Some Bible scholars state that Ham was a cursed people and they were destined to be servants of their brothers. The above statement seems to dismiss this myth.

{This information came directly from the <u>Original African Heritage Study Bible</u>:

Dr. Seaton was a prominent leader in the African Methodist Episcopal Church who wrote in 1895 displaying considerable knowledge about the Bible, the location of ancient religious sites, and the significance of many biblical characters. In fact, he made several field trips to Palestine. In his major work a volume of 443 pages of text notes, maps, and illustrations, he provides extensive descriptions of tombs, villages, and other ancient sites, which he visited. It is noteworthy that Seaton's study displays a profound awareness of racism among the "bona fide" Bible scholars of his day. He could have benefited greatly from systematic historical critical engagement with the biblical text in its original languages.} [11]

This is according to the <u>Original African Heritage Study Bible</u>. However, from the Egyptian skulls, it has been estimated that at least one-third of the Egyptian population was clearly Black. We should remember that in Chapter 10 of Genesis, all of the groups of the world are described as having been derived from one source and that was Noah, and his family (descendants of Adam and Eve). According to the researchers of the Original African Study Bible, Noah is alluded to as indeed being a man of color.

If, then, this information is factual, all of the present people on earth after the Flood had the same beginnings. African slaves brought with them to America the belief system called "African Traditional Religion." They came into America with their own form of religion or Christianity, which included close and extensive bonds of kinship that endured beyond the grave and elaborate public ceremonies for relating to gods and various ancestors; while still realizing or having a consciousness of one Supreme Being—God.

Though the African continent is very large, it was divided into various countries each with its own culture, languages, dialects, and belief systems. Therefore, the African Traditional Religion's success in North America was not as great as in Latin America. The slaves attempted to communicate with each other by grunts and groans, and by showing one another by hand signals similar to sign language to convey what they were trying to say. Each new batch of slaves had to be introduced to the form of communication that the slaves had among themselves. Some were able to keep alive in their hearts the old religious ways; when they were alone in the "dead of night," they would steal away; quietly down by the water to pray and mainly praying to God for their freedom.

Remember that none of the Africans necessarily came from the same language groups or the same tribes. Therefore, they could not understand each other, but they could all understand the drums—they were universal. The drums were a form of communication that all Africans could understand. The Europeans forbid the slaves to play the drums. The main commonality that the slaves shared was their distressful conditions and sufferings created by this strange-looking "blue-eyed white skinned creature." This could be cited as "cultural shock."

Stressed daily by the pressures of slavery, the Africans' power for coping with enslavement (like believing that he had the ability to fly in order to avoid whippings or other abuses) is perhaps what some psychologists would term or call the use of a form of mental power in order to survive. These and other methods were employed by some African slaves to help them in their dire moments of crisis. Christianity, in its anti-slavery version presented a slavery-hating God who controlled the universe and intended to liberate the slaves in His own good time. Christianity was no longer just a White religion in America: Slaves had discovered a form of Christianity with a friendly brown face. Blended with beliefs and mysteries of Africa, this was turned inward to form a state of well -being; bringing them a sense of power, and comfort; to keep struggling in their horrendous situation. It is apparent that Christianity played a major part in the survival of the Black group in America. However, many older people remembered a different time, or their parents kept telling them of how it used to be in their homeland (Africa).

Africa was remembered as the place of freedom and mysterious power. African American-born slaves tended to view native Africans as a people like themselves even though there were great variations in American Christianity based upon the European pattern of worship. (Author's note: The Queen of England also endorsed slavery, as did all the powers that be, the economic aspect of buying and selling humans was very profitable.)

However, the growth of Christianity among slaves did not exclude the memory of influences from Africa. For these Black Americans, Christianity provided the large perspective on life, death, and their very destiny, while the African heritage provided concrete ways of dealing with everyday problems relating to health, interpersonal relations, and the natural world. Both the African and Christian Traditional Religion were prevalent within the African American community. The Black Church has historically been a stalwart and major support of the African-American. Black Churches continued to flourish and more members joined as time passed.

The slave's form of religion most of the time served the master's interest, but for many slaves, it fueled the resistance, that shaped their religion. Slaves came to believe that their religion took in greater forces on behalf of their humanity than did their masters' religions. Whether or not the slaves were able to resist openly, they could in their hearts, knowing that God intended for them to have freedom.

There were many problems even for Blacks attempting to serve the Lord.

The main reason for the denial of Blacks to congregate together was based on the fear of insurrections, or the plotting to run away. And further, if Blacks were taught brotherhood and equality for all mankind before God, they would not be content to remain in bondage. This also means that Whites did not feel comfortable when large groups of Blacks congregated together. There had been many insurrections against the White masters throughout the south.

So it was necessary to lie to them, and to remind them that God wanted them to be in servitude, "Servants obey your master, and this is the will of God." Of course, this was added with other quotes out of context from the Bible. Even at that, slaves knew that God wanted them to be free. The White owners had to find a method to protect their rights to own slaves and to remain in positions of power over them. The masters would also tell Black preachers to reiterate the same types of sermons. To ensure that this was done, a White minister would be in the church to make sure no meaningful truth was spoken.

Slaves believed that Jesus was the Messiah-King who would liberate them, as Moses had liberated the Israelites. And, Jesus was also the Savior who would carry them to freedom in heaven. In the slaves' mind, the slave-holder's religion was hopelessly corrupt, for it (the White man's religion) favored slave holding. The masters' hypocritical religion would not protect them from God's sure punishment. Meanwhile, the followers of God's true religion should live as God meant from the beginning. For many slaves, this meant a resistance as a Christian duty. This included flight, sabotage, malingering, or whatever the slave could do in regard to halt the progress. The average slave day was from sunup to sundown, with maybe a day off on Sunday or at least part of Sunday off.

{According to Franklin & Moss:
The invitation to Negroes to attend the White Churches, the acceptance of which bordered on compulsion, did not represent a movement in the direction of increased brotherhood. Rather, it was a method that white employed to keep a closer eye on the slave. It was believed that too many of the conspiracies had been planned in religious gatherings and that such groups gave the abolitionist an opportunity to distribute incendiary ideas and literature. When Bishop Atkinson of North Carolina raises the question "Where are our Negroes," he not only implied that

they were in Churches other than the Episcopal Church but that they were beyond the restraining influence of the conservative element of the white society. When the slaves attended the Churches of the planters; they usually sat either in the gallery or in a special section. The earliest examples of racial segregation are to be found in the Churches.} [12]

Such fears proved accurate, for many of the most obedient and influential slaves had a keen understanding of the difference between the gospel of pro- slavery preachers and the Christian scriptures, message of divine punishment for oppressors and liberation for the faithful. Christianity was a freedom-based religion.

Now exactly what should be done with all of the freed Blacks after 1863 and 1865. The early White Americans were faced with a very grave situation. Some wanted to send all the Blacks back to Africa, and some Blacks wanted to return. However, most Blacks decided that they had been in America for so long and had built this country; they wanted to stay. Blacks did not want to forget their relatives that had died in America, which also added reasons for them to stay.

Some Christians participated in the "Back to Africa" movement, and there were several trips made to Africa from America at this time. Lincoln and others felt that it was the only thing to do. Since Blacks were no longer considered to be property, under White dominance, they had no further use in America. Unfortunately, this was not very successful, because few Blacks felt an alliance to Africa after being in America for hundreds of years. They had forgotten their languages, and dialects. Most Whites wanted all Blacks to return to Africa to rid the country of their existence.

While most Whites maltreated Blacks, America was still the only home that they knew. The former slave owners had no further use for the newly freed Blacks. However, Marcus Garvey was a strong advocate for the "Back to Africa" Movement in the 1920s. He was a proud Jamaican, and he owned ships. These ships were used to transport Blacks back to Africa. This movement was largely unsuccessful in transporting large populations of freed Blacks back to Africa. However, some Blacks went back to the homeland. The sad truth is that some freed Blacks were not respectful to the Native Africans that they encountered. This movement was further approved of by the governmental administration in Washington, D.C.

Blacks that went back formed a new country in Africa that was called Liberia. The capitol was Monrovia, named after President James Monroe. It was just another colony of the United States. It was interesting to find that the Black Americans had the tendency to treat the native Africans similar to the way Whites had treated them in America. This shows the mistreatment for long periods of time become a "way of life."

However, the U.S. Government put in place a program designed to assist the newly freed Blacks and poor Whites. This was called the Freedmen's Bureau. This effort provided health and hospitals, built some schools, and many Blacks learned to read and write. This program was short lived, and did little to help many displaced and unemployed Blacks. The Bureau tried to negotiate fair wages for Blacks.

Reconstruction was a short lived project; the Federal Government withdrew the federal troops from the South and left White Southerners in charge of their lives and the lives of their Blacks. They had the ability to decide what they wanted to do with the freed Blacks. The vote that was given to Blacks was quickly taken away. Many poll taxes, and other blocks were put in place to keep Blacks from voting, and from having a decent quality of life. Whites were determined to be superior, and to remain in power. The various hate groups arose about this time, including the Ku Klux Klan. The Southerners also came up with Black Codes, which attempted to put most Blacks back into slavery. This was to the dismay and horror of the newly freed Blacks who were left defenseless and at the mercy of their former masters. It did not matter the abuse and treatment, this was home for countless Blacks.

It was a blessing that most Black historical parents decided to stay in America. Blacks were determined to survive because of the sacrifices previously made by their forefathers. America was their country too, and they were determined to stay here. After all, many Black people had fought in every war, died for democracy, and yet, it eluded them back home in America. Remembering how this country was built from the blood and sweat of countless Black persons, Blacks had a right to be here to be treated with equally and justice.

Again, the Church was all that Blacks had to depend upon. The Black minister now no longer had to say what he was told by the overseer or the master. The White man was no longer directly in charge anymore. Blacks were free to worship God as they saw fit and it pleased them to worship in spirit and in truth, with a joyful noise and shouting "hallelujah!" The Bible was read and discussed as the preacher decided with the help of the Holy Ghost what was needed to benefit the members. Some Ministers say 'being led by the spirit' or the 'Holy Ghost.' Today, there is a large difference between the services in a predominately all White church and Black Church. And as stated earlier, ironically, it is a very segregated time, in this integrated nation. Some Whites were trying to work together; however, it was basically to keep an eye on Blacks. This type of "spying" led to distrust by Blacks of Whites and their motivations.

Problems arose between the Baptist; there was not only the conflict between the progressives and the conservatives, but also a struggle between Whites and Blacks in general. In many localities, Whites tried to control Black Baptist associations and conventions, much to the distress of the Black leaders. When Blacks were refused the privilege of participating in the management of the American Baptist Publication Society, under pressure from Southern Churches, refused to accept contributions from Blacks to obtain Sunday school literature a serious breach developed between the two groups.

It was very sad that these two groups could not even agree on the fundamental beliefs that Blacks had a right to have ownership of their own Churches and their learning materials. This was undue interference by some White Christians. Even the conservatives yielded to the demands of the more enlightened members that the church; that served as an agency for the improvement of the social and moral conditions among Negroes. Churches in New York, Detroit, Chicago, St. Louis, and other cities engaged in similar activities. This progressive development served not only to contribute to the improvement of conditions in urban communities, but also to attract better-trained young men to the ministry from the Black churches.

{Franklin & Moss stated:
The white Methodists of New York had much the same attitude toward their Negro fellows, as did their counterpart in Philadelphia. The result was a withdrawal of Negroes from the John Street Methodist Episcopal Zion Church, and the establishment of the African Methodist Episcopal Zion Church in 1796. Leading in this movement were Peter Williams, James Varick, elected the first Bishop in 1822, George Collins, and Christopher Rush. They could find no one in either the Episcopal or the Methodist church that would ordain and consecrate their elders, and finally hey had to do it themselves. Overcoming schisms within and opposition without, the Church was sufficiently stable by 1822 to elect a bishop, and to set up a program of expansion. The same trend toward independent organizations manifested itself among the Baptists. In 1809 thirteen Negro members of a white Baptist church in Philadelphia were dismissed to form a Church of their own. Under the leadership of Reverend Burrows, a former slave, it became an important institution among the Negroes of that community. The Negro Baptists of Boston, under the leadership of Reverend Thomas Paul, organized their Church in 1809. At about the same time, he was assisting in organizing the Church in New York that later came to be known as the Abyssinian Baptist Church. In each instance organization was brought about as a result of the separation of Blacks from White congregations. } [13]

(This author cannot fathom why any Black would want to be Methodist or Baptist rather than a Quaker; considering all the abuse and maltreatment that came along with some of the other denominations).

> {Franklin & Moss continues:
> Once the planters were convinced that conversion did not have the effect of emancipating their slaves, they sought to use the Church as an agency for maintaining the institution of slavery. Ministers were encouraged to instruct the slaves along the lines of obedience and subservience. Bishops and high church officials were not above owning slaves and fostering the continuation of slavery.
> ….The Presbyterians and Quakers seemed to have been the most liberal in their attitude toward Negroes, but they were not the large slaveholders. The latter were to be found in the Episcopal Church on the Atlantic seaboard and in the Baptist and Methodist churches in the cotton kingdom. In the last three decades before the Civil War the church became one of the strongest allies of the proslavery element. Slaves who had found refuge and solace in the religious instructions of the white clergy had reason to believe that an enemy that had once befriended them now trapped them.} [14]

The so-called freedom promised to the slaves did not happen, in other words a Christian or not slavery was going to remain. In fact the Church was one of slavery's main supports.

The major denominations that Blacks belonged to were/are the Baptist, Methodist, and The Church of God in Christ; Most Blacks if polled would belong to one of these Churches. The AME, and AMEZ also tend to have a large Black following in recent years. At one time it was reportedly said that if slaves became "Christian," then they would be given their freedom, or some freedoms. Well, it did not take very long to see that this was just another "trick" by the White man. As thousands upon thousands of slaves were baptized, not many were treated any differently than before. Whites had stated that slaves would get special treatment, would be able to keep their families together, and to have more time off. None of these things happened for the majority of slaves in America. There are always exceptions to any rule, and this case is no different. There were a few slaves, who upon accepting Christianity, survived better—but this was not true for the majority of slaves.

Although Church membership was increasing, organized religious bodies were going through a period that was as critical for Black as for Whites. Its leadership, however, was being effectively challenged by rising progressive elements, which refused to accept the crude notions of Biblical interpretation and the "grotesque vision of the hereafter" portrayed by the conservatives. Educated Negroes began to reject the church as the agency of salvation and turned their attention more and more to the immediate problems at hand. They demanded a change in management that would give them more in keeping with their improved intellectual levels. Frequently, the progressives withdrew from Baptist and Methodist denominations and joined with Congregational, Presbyterian, Episcopalian, and Catholic churches, some of which seemed to have more flexible attitudes toward the reforms upon which the progressives insisted.

The first in a movement away from "traditional" Black Churches was the Black Muslims in the 1950s and early 1960s. The Black Muslims were a sect based loosely on the Mohammedan faith and advocating strict separation of the races. Prior to the 1960's the words: Black or Negro: dirty, soiled or stained with dirt, without moral goodness; whereas the meanings of White or Caucasian: pure as the driven snow, morally pure, innocent. This was the manner in which these terms were listed in the dictionary of old. No wonder no one wanted to be called Black; the words were always considered to be negative. The terminology for White was always so positive. But, who wrote the dictionaries? When reality hit, and the publishers were enlightened then the wording was a bit more palatable for both groups. All of a sudden it was time for Black Pride. This was the period of time when James Brown was singing, "I'm Black and I'm Proud." Prior to the new burst of Blackness, it was difficult for some Blacks to admit or wanted to be called Black. (Because of the connotations associated with being Black in America (the old dictionary was a good example of negativity). (This authors' note: For verification take a look at an old dictionary and read what Black meant, or Negro, compared to White, or Caucasian and their assigned meanings).

Other movements went back to the ancient African tribal religions that held sacred many gods in nature. However, even with these beliefs, they always knew and believed in the one almighty God.

With the idea of Black Consciousness popularized through music, some of the traditional Christian denomination leaders began speaking out for a change. It was necessary; if Dr. King had remained silent concerning the "unjust laws" the progress that was gained towards equality would never have been started. Interestingly, many of the clergy felt that Dr. King being a minister of God was out of place working for civil rights. Who was more qualified to be concerned? Men of God have made many changes in history. It is ironic that Christianity was used to "keep Blacks under control during slavery;" and for many years following slavery. All of these hundreds of years, Blacks suffered under the guise of following the word of the Lord; which was being misinterpreted and often used to keep Blacks servile and in bondage. What a conflict? (This author' notes: Believes that this was the reason so many young Blacks converted to the Muslim religion in the 1960's).

In recent years, there are ministers, such as Cone and Cleage who have studied and researched Black History as it relates to the Holy Bible. They have established what is called a "Black Theology." This is one of the latest in religious directions for some of the "modern-day" Blacks in America. (Author's note: not all Blacks ascribe to Cone and Cleage but they have a right to their beliefs and this is why they are included in this book).

{In fact, Minister Cleage calls his church the Church of the Black Madonna:
In the chapel area, instead of the traditionally stained-glass window, there is a large portrait of the Black Madonna and child painted very Black, with distinct Negroid features. This is quite startling for many people, both Black and White, who have nev-

er seen the usual paintings of these figures 'colored' anything but "White."} [14]

Note: {In 1986, this author went to Paris, France and saw the statute of the Black Madonna and Child and took a picture of the statute, this was a wonderful sight to see). In some countries in Europe, the churches have always had the Black statues in their Churches; this included many dark figures of Christ, his mother Mary, and the nativity scenes. America has most religious artifacts painted "white." This has been the custom historically to do so in America. In the 1960's some Churches had a 'brown' Jesus. Catholic Churches began to have darker statues in their sanctuaries.

Ultimately, religion has become an expression and celebration. Some Churches have a "Gospel Choir" that sings old Black spirituals and upbeat music to celebrate their joy in the Lord. This interpreted religion offers hope for a better life, and future for their children. Man was created in the beginning in God's own image and likeness. The promise was to accept His son and then look forward to being with God for eternity. (This is what some Europeans did to God; they made Him white). The original brown/black God was given European features and therefore, their God looked very much like the persons who painted him, thereby, personalizing their white God.

{Some other ideas according to Cone stated as follows:
This means that to love black people, he has taken on black oppressed existence becoming one of us. He (Jesus) is black because he loves us; and he loves us because we are black.} [15]

(Author's note: This has been seen as reverse racism; however, this author maintains that a people without wealth, power, or prestige, cannot be racist! In other words –some words may be harsh, but there are no consequences that Blacks can levy upon Whites in America to make a difference in their lives. As a collective group some Blacks may be wealthy, but it is sparse, there is no real power or prestige within the Black community to wield against Whites in any form. In other words Blacks can do nothing to withhold employment, housing or anything that really matter for a people to survive. Without wealth, power, or prestige no one group can harm any other group. Blacks may talk and feel aggressive but it is mostly talk. And that is a very good thing to be able to express oneself and share opinions this is very healthy.)

Many people will have a very hard time aligning themselves with such drastic statements made by Cone, but yet, ministers like Cone and Cleage agree that these measures were necessary in order to counteract the oppression of "White racism," even as it relates to Christianity. These ministers think that all Churches should adhere to their philosophy or belief system. This theology has been considered to be radical by many Blacks, and

Mainly the Black Muslims and some of their teachings have utilized the following for these ideas. The further think that Black people must realize that a White Jesus' picture has no place in the Black community. Blacks should replace Him with a Black Messiah, as Albert Cleage would say: (Note: this author realizes that not all people (or all Blacks) agree with Cleage).

{Cleage continues:
Unfortunately, American White Theology has not been involved in the struggle for Black Liberation…and neither has all Black Americans. White oppressors or White Theology has given religious sanction to the genocide of (Indians) Native Americans and the enslavement of Black people….}[16]

Similar to the way the churches sanctioned slavery, it was profitable for the planters and the clergy as some owned slaves and reaped the benefits.

{According to Cleage:
From the very beginning to the present day, American White Theological thought has been "patriotic," either by defining the theological task independently of black suffering (the liberal northern approach) or by defining Christianity as compatible with white racism) the conservative southern approach –that

is. In both cases, theology becomes a servant of the state, and that can only mean death to black people. It is little wonder they conclude that an increasing number of young blacks are finding it difficult to be black and also to be identified with traditional theological thought forms of "traditional Christianity."} [17]

And the mistreatment by the clergy lends credence to the feelings of many Black males in the 1960's that perhaps God was for the White man and not for people of color.

Since the early 1960s, this has been a dilemma for Black young people- what to believe in and what is true? Why do images of God not reflect a man of color? Blacks in the 1960s and '70s were looking for answers and they were not accepting the traditional old weary answers from the previous generations. Older Blacks are seen as "Uncle Toms, too old-fashioned, not being with "what is happening." (This authors' note: If the God of the Holy Bible was good enough for my ancestors He is good enough for me)!

Young Blacks wanted to try something new, and Black Theology was that "something" for many Black people.

{According to James Cone:
There are two reasons why Black Theology is a Christian theology and possibly the only expression of Christian theology in America. First, there can be no theology of the gospel, which does not arise from an oppressed community. This is so because God in Christ has revealed himself as a God whose righteousness is inseparable from the weak and helpless in human society. The goal of Black Theology is to interpret God's activity as he is related to the oppressed black community. } [18]

(This author's opinion is that Jesus had compassion upon the poor and the downtrodden, no matter their ethnic groups or color.)

{Cone comments further:
Black theology is Christian theology because it centers on Jesus Christ. There can be no Christian theology that does not have Jesus Christ as its point of departure. Though Black Theology

affirms the Black condition as the primary reality, which must be dealt with, this does not mean that it denies the absolute revelation of God in Jesus Christ. Rather it affirms it. Unlike White Theology that tends to make the Christ-event an abstract, intellectual idea, Black Theology believes that the Black community itself is precisely where Christ is at work. Most Blacks would like to believe that this is true, as many lives in America are besieged with problems stemming from an unjust system. }[19]

It is hoped that eventually White and Black Americans alike will be convinced that American Blacks have an historical background. And they have made sufficient contributions to the development of the human race, and have participated in the findings and in the origination of the birthplace of all of mankind. These roots are in the Holy Bible. Although, there was evidence that Blacks in the Bible that dates back prior to the 18th century, it has been only in the past 25 years that Black scholars and ministers have made major breakthroughs on the subject that has been ignored or suppressed by White religious authorities throughout modern history.

Most of the modern research, however, is based upon the findings of other Black historians like William Leo Hansberry and W.E.B. Dubois, who identified major Black biblical characters more than 50 years ago. Only a few persons listened to them, and now many researchers, historians, and ministers have validated the former information, using the Holy Bible as a book that God has written as a "map" for His followers.

There can be little doubt, of course, that the Caucasian group implemented and made major "psychological" transformations on Blacks; during and after slavery. Some Whites thoroughly convinced Blacks that they were inferior, no good, shiftless, and lazy. After years of this type of negativity it becomes ingrained into the mind of the person. It took years to behave in a negative manner and it will take time to begin to behave in a positive manner. In spite of the information to the contrary, actually Blacks built this country with their blood, sweat, and tears from far too many years of strenuous work, and under horrendous conditions.

Once a people "buy" into "stereotypes," they begin to "internalize" them, and then it is very difficult to turn this self-negativity into something positive. It must be understood that it took many years for Blacks to get the second-class "mind set," and it will take the same amount of time or more for the truth to bring about the needed change.

Some of the fastest growing churches were the Baptists, Presbyterians, and the Quakers. After the Civil War, the Catholic Churches, along with the AME and the AME Zion Churches, began to grow with larger numbers of Blacks as members. Please know that, major churches did little or nothing to stop slavery. Sure there were always a few ministers that would speak out for the abolition of slavery, but their voices were not heard. John Wesley was one minister whose voice was heard and he violently protested against the evils of slavery.

(The Author's note: In fact, some of ministers reaped benefits because their parishioners were able to pay more money into the church if they had lots of slave. There was only one Church that did many things to help slaves and that was the Quakers, or the Friends Church. It amazes this author as to why most Blacks are not Quakers. Perhaps that is because most Blacks are not cognizant of the true history concerning the Quaker churches and their major contributions to the freedom of slaves.)

Slaves had a "spiritual connection" with God that helped them to bear the harsh tenets of slavery. This connection helped them to use imagery to survive slavery.

There are three frequently used terms: Spirituality, Christianity, and religion as defined in Webster's Dictionary:

- <u>Spirituality</u>: Something that is an ecclesiastical law that belongs to the church or to a cleric as such. Author's note: Slaves used it to survive.
- <u>Christianity</u>: As the religion derived from Jesus Christ, based on the Bible as sacred scripture, and professed by Eastern, Roman Catholic, and Protestant bodies.
- <u>Religion</u>: The service and worship of God or the supernatural. Commitment or devotion to religious faith or observance. A personal set or institutionalized system of religious attitudes, beliefs, and practices.

Black religions, often embrace spiritually, and it is very essential. Some Blacks tend to be "in touch," if you will, with the "higher power-"God! This spirituality or communicating with God can be done prior to sleeping, while driving in one's car, or when one is at work. In fact, this communication between God and man can happen anywhere and anytime, not just in a Church building. To be exact, this is the foundational "root" for the church and the mind-set of the Black American. Without this concept of spirituality, there would not be any true religious meanings for most Black Americans.

This is the main basis for the particular form of religious expression that can be found in "African American Churches" throughout the United States. As a matter of fact, most Black churches tend to be "louder" than other Churches; because of the methods of worshiping and praising The Lord Jesus Christ. Some, however, are more pronounced than others, but spirituality is the foundation of the Black belief system.

In the 1970s, approximately 18 million Blacks belonged to various Christian denominations in the United States. However, in an effort to clearly show their growing feelings into spiritual realms, some Blacks moved away from the traditional religions that were symbolized by a White Mother, and child. And have begun to seek emotional as well as social solidarity in other forms of religions. As stated before, one such movement was the Black Muslims. Another movement went back to the ancient African tribal religions that worshiped many sacred gods in nature. But, the majority of Africans believed not in polytheistic forms of worship, but rather in a monotheistic God.

Even the worshipers of the many gods knew and believed in the One Supreme God. Within the traditional Christian denominations, there were religious leaders speaking out for a change. It is not to say that Blacks do not believe in God, but that it's the way in which they formally worshiped which needs to be shifted to include their spirituality, and to realize that God is of color, and that the Black man was shaped and formed in God's own image.

Many Black Church leaders reveal a firm commitment to a common societal vision, namely a society that acknowledges as significant neither race, color, nationality, class, nor station. Many have been unaware that their vision has been identical with the so-called melting pot theory that has been implicit in the America consciousness both as fact and norm throughout much of the twentieth century. However, as my brother previously mentioned Sunday remains separate and segregated, at 11:00 am. Also as mentioned earlier there has been some mingling of the various groups especially African Americans and Caucasians attend integrated churches, but again this pattern is not largely seem in most cities throughout America.

{Paris stated:
…Most black church leaders reveal a firm commitment to a common societal vision, namely a society that acknowledges as significant neither race, color, nationality, class, nor station. Many have been unaware that their vision has been identical with the so-called melting pot theory that has been implicit in the American consciousness both as fact and norm throughout much of the twentieth century.} [20]

This theory did not last very long, because America is still a very "color conscious nation." No matter how many laws there are people are still going to judge by the color of the skin, rather than as Dr. King so eloquently said by the character of a person.

{Paris continues:
Recently many sociologists, Black and White, have abandoned the melting-pot theory in favor of various theories of cultural pluralism, thus setting terms of the present debate. The assimilations implied by the melting pot-theory aims at homogeneous culture, the full realization of which is thought by some to be impossible as long as a visible racial factor is present. Theories of cultural pluralism, on the other hand, emphasize the importance of inclusion while affirming various differences of race, ethnicity, and religion}. [21]

Cultural pluralism has been seen as the best of all theories to date. It provides for inclusion and also acknowledges the various ethnicities and religions that may be present.

However, man has decided which people are important on earth and which ones are not, as this book has attempted to point out by the many examples given. Recently many sociologists, Black and White, have abandoned the melting-pot theory in favor of various theories of cultural pluralism, thus setting terms of the present debate. The assimilation implied by the melting-pot theory aims at homogeneous culture, the full realization of which is thought by some to be impossible as long as a visible racial factor is present. Theories of cultural pluralism, on the other hand, emphasize the importance of inclusion while affirming various differences of race, ethnicity, and religion. Hopefully, soon the tern "race" will be completely removed. Different-looking Humans Homo sapiens are what makes America the beautiful patchwork quilt that she is.

The term human is a combination of two words; most people never take the time to consider the meanings of the words that we use.

{According to Anthony Browder:
The term human can be divided into two basic words, hue and man. This literally means "man from the humus" (soil, the earth), a fancy way of saying Black man or man of color (hue), which describe the kinds of man that evolved into human.} [22]

Browder is correct with his interpretation of the word human. Evidentially, this portion of the word human (hue) relates to color from ebony to ivory.

{Browder continues with information about color:
Basic genetics states that all colors are contained within melanin or dark cells and white cells contain no color.' Simply put, it is possible for a race of brown, yellow, and white people to be produced from the cells of black people. But it is impossible for a race of black people to be produced from the cells of brown, yellow, or white races of people.} [23]

It would seem that if any group evolved then it was the "fairer" group according to Browder. It would seem that black is the original and all other groups came from the one group.

{Browder further states.
'All the early references speak of man as coming from the earth. Adam, the biblical first man, is a word, which means "man of the earth." The original name for Egypt was Kemit, which means "people of the Black land."' The ancient Kemitian word Africa literally meant the "birthplace" of humanity.} [24]

If the Bible for instance had been translated correctly the first time, then it would not be necessary to have had to go back and find the correct words and their meanings to bring out a balanced version, such as the Original African Heritage Study Bible. We have many talented researchers and historians who have helped to show the way for truth to be revealed.

{According to the Cress Theory:
What then necessitated changing the image of Black Jesus and Black Mary to White Christ and Mary? To answer this question, we must return to the most fundamental fact in the existence of the global white collective: White-skinned people initially were the mutant albino of Black people in Africa. These White-skinned people were recognized as having a disease; just as today's modern science of genetics refers to the conditions of albi-

nism (the lack of pigmentation) as a genetic deficiency disease. The pigmented population shunned the albinos or the fairer skinned people banded together. The lighter skinned people were banned from the living among the pigmentation group.

Authors' notes: This theory is just about as reliable as any in written history. When a group is given a chance to write their own history, this kind of information will be forthcoming. Europeans for the most part wrote History and it certainly identified their heritage and their "so-called" beginnings}. [25]

This theory seems to have merit if indeed all colors evolved from black, according to Cress.

{Cress continues:
Eventually, they (light skinned people) had to migrate northward to remove themselves from the intense African sun- rays. Migrating northward from Africa, the albino populations eventually settled in the area of the world now referred to as Europe. There, they increased in number and eventually returned to conquer the people of color in Africa, Asia, and the rest of the world. They returned with the idea that they would conquer and no longer think of themselves as the rejected and diseased population; instead, they would think of themselves, in compensation, as the superior and supreme supermen and look upon all skin-pigmented peoples as the "genetic inferiors."} [26]

The "lacking" or the group without color was jealous and perhaps felt inferior, and it seems that often the "lighter" group members were ostracized from the other groups of color. That could cause hostility.

{Cress states further:
With the necessity for such a compensatory ideology and concept of self as superior, the White psyche could tolerate no concept of anything higher than the White self—not even God. Thus, when the concept of the Son of God was formulated, in their thinking, the "Son" eventually took the form of a White man, which by brain-computer logic would mean that God him-

self had to be a White man. Thus, the White collective, in logical reality, is not worshiping any force beyond itself. } [27]

If Whites had treated others with respect perhaps we would not have such dilemma that has lasted until today.

{Cress continues with her examination of the White collective psyche:

Further, it is apparent that the collective White psyche felt anger towards God for bequeathing them with what is now understood as a genetic defect, namely white skin. In turn, they have spawned the thinking that doubts and denies the existence of God. Thus, they have conceived of themselves as being at war with nature, which is the reflection of God. They function as though they are in contest with God and try to out-create God.} [28]

It would seem that if any group should be angry it would be the group "left out of the mix" so to speak. If Whites are indeed angry with God that might be one of the reasons for so much bloodshed and killing of many people world-wide. By being aggressive and dominant they figured out how to be gods themselves!

The Egyptians, Ethiopians, and Jews were the principle people in the Holy Bible. The Bible is multiracial and multicultural. The known world was in the Bible at the original time that it was written. The references are heavily people of color in the Bible.

In the years following the reformation, the Europeans pictured the Bible characters as being European. In the early days of the Bible period, there was no concern about color prejudice. It seems that most people were of color to one degree or another.

It's hard to imagine that in our racist society today that we could ever have a society without it that would, however, be an ideal society as it should be. Nevertheless, it is very gratifying to have a correct translation of the Holy Bible that shows all people portrayed the way they were meant to be. It is understand that many people, both Black and White, will reject its message and meanings entirely. That is because of the "mind set" of some Americans.

There first be a deletion of the prior messages of negativity that has been given to Blacks for over four hundred years. It will take time for some, but for others it was a revelation that has been long overdue. Hopefully, there were some things that were unknown that are now revealed. With information now available some parts of history can now be corrected. Some of the authors included in this book were to show that Black people had their own opinions about early history and many researched to find out what they did find. Most historical information used in this book is grounded in fact. The Black Church has always been the stalwart of strength for the Black families throughout slavery up to this present time.

All Christians can thank the contributors of <u>The Original African Heritage Study Bible</u> for their great contribution to the knowledge and research of the truth. We must remember also that our God has no respect for one group; except of course, the children of Israel. It is wonderful to know that God is not a respecter of persons He loves His entire "rainbow" of children equally and has prepared a place for each one of us that believe and trust in Him. This world is not our home and one day we will each leave this earth with nothing, which is the way we entered and that is precisely the way we will leave it! The only things in life worth having are the things we did for others, the Bible says when we do for the least of these we did it unto the Lord Jesus Christ!

"I will lift up mine eyes unto the hills, from whence cometh my help."
-Psalms 121:1

THE CONCLUSION

This book has been one in which the information used was re-searched over many years. It is hoped that this study will broaden the vision of some, peak the curiosity of others, and inform all concerning the many discoveries and explorations that Black Americans and their ancestors have made to early civilization. This study has taken the reader on a journey from "the creation" of humankind to this present time period.

This author could not have written this book without including my Lord and Saviour Jesus Christ. Included are His birth and His life without which this author would not have been able to complete this book; or have the patience to work on it for several years. All thanks and praises go to Him my "everything."

This book was written primarily because of Chapter III., Civilization in Africa. Please read it and then re-read it again, this was the main reason for writing this in one place

This author has found "nuggets" in many places but they needed to be put them altogether. It took years of research to find what was written about the African input. As previously stated I am grateful that the Greeks wrote down the historical information and gave credit to the African nation.

This author is further grateful to Joel Augustus Rogers,' Lerone Bennett, Jr., Ivan Van Sertima, Dr. Leo Wiener, Drs. L.S.B. Leakey and wife Mary for their man contributions to make sure that this valuable information was passed on and not lost. There are too many authors to list them all here, but they have also made deep impressions on the intellect of the astute reader.

Importantly, this book was not intended to put other groups down or to say that Blacks are better than others, but it was to show that because of racism and deception, the African/Black contributions have been left out of history books and denied in the Bible. But, God, in His infinite wisdom, would not allow the White man to fully negate the Black presence, in the scriptures or in history.

The "people of color" today, who now call themselves either Black or African American, have made major differences. It is about time that Blacks were able to "label" themselves. It is also imperative that the "real history" be told, Africans have contributed greatly to the very beginnings of civilization. Africans were inventors, scientists, mathematicians, scholars, ministers, teachers, in the past and present.

It seems that little has been written in history books about the many times the Greeks wrote about the "gifts" of the Africans, among those according to John G. Jackson were Herodotus, Diodorus, Strabo, Pliny, and Homer. Van Sertima wrote about the University of Timbuktu, among others, which had many great scholars, which included doctors, judges, and priests. It seems that the Greeks were determined to write about what they had learned over the years from Africa.

For many readers, this book will be very "hard" to digest, but for others, it will be a "cool breeze of refreshment." With God's grace, it is hoped that each man will learn to live in peace and harmony with his fellow man regardless of race, creed, or religious beliefs. This obligation to love each person holds especially true for all Christians on earth. We must remember these motivational words from the scriptures, "And ye shall know the truth, and the truth shall make you free."

This author: Went on the Internet to glean additional information on "Race."

This is the latest it comes from the 2000 Census:

Definitions:

White: People having origins in any of the original peoples of Europe, the Middle East, or North Africa
Black or African
American: People having origins in any of the Black racial groups of Africa

American Indian and
Alaska Native: People having origins in any of the original people of North and South America (including Central America), and who maintain tribal affiliation or community attachment.

Asian: People having origins in any of the original peoples of the Far East, Southeast Asia, or the Indian subcontinent.

Native Hawaiian and
Other Pacific Islander: People having origins in any of the original peoples of Hawaii, Guam, Samoa, or other Pacific Islands.

(These "racial" categories were established for the U.S. Census Bureau by the Office of Management and Budget in October 1999)
Please note:
Latino /or/ Hispanic: People that are now considered to be an "Ethnic" Group rather than a racial group.
People coming from Mexico and/or Southwest section of the United States are not classified as a "racial" group. (This author's note: It is too bad that the other categories are not classified as just "humans)."

This author's ending notes:
In the twenty-first century, African or Black Americans are refusing to be devalued, dehumanized, and ignored. This author would like to make a direct challenge especially, to the parents of Black youth,

to teach them about The Lord Jesus Christ. Then teach Godly values and morals in your home, by example. Remind your children about the need for excellence in education. And, be sure that they are taught about Black History whether in a private setting or in the public schools. This is a prerequisite for them to become all that they are capable of becoming. Black youth need guidance and support along with lots of love and understanding. The many discoveries and inventions made by Blacks in Africa and in America have given many needed implements for survival to all men throughout the world. The world owes a great debt of gratitude to the Black man.

Blacks must reject the notion of being "cool" and all of the "street jive," which includes some of the negative "rap songs." Many of these songs are demeaning to Black women, being called out of their names, and being put down, portraying them as 'hookers, sluts, and whores.' All of these young men and women had a mother surely they would not want anyone to say these type words about or around their loved ones, be it mother, sister or other female family member. Another main ingredient would be the need to attend church together, and remember the Creator always!

The Legacy will hopefully answer many of the questions that have not been previously answered in other books or in school. **Looking back while moving forward** seemed to be the ideal title for this book. It is also hoped that this will be a "Bridge From the Past to the Present" and will not be seen as a negative journey, but a positive one. This author is deeply indebted to the contributor's from **The Original African Heritage Bible**. We all need to thank God for His goodness and His protection that has enabled African Americans/ Blacks to survive. May all who read this book appreciate the knowledge and the contributions made throughout the years by people that are now called Blacks or African- Americans; let us not forget our White" brothers as well as our Latino brothers who have written about Africans and the people who are now known as African Americans. Also, Blacks desperately need to eliminate the negatives and focus upon the positives in life. May this "new" directional journey; of enlightenment prevail as we as a Christian nation, move forward together into the future!

This book was not completed until after the election of 2009, and America elected the first African American. The election of President Barack Obama is a history- making event. Obama's speech on 28 Aug 08 was exactly 45 years from when Dr. Martin Luther King, Jr., spoke in Washington, D.C. Dr. King had a "Dream." It took years but in this author's lifetime was able to see the dream come to fruition! To God be the glory, all things in due season will come to pass. This historic event will be forever engraved into American History, and it will prove that Americans can unite and work together regardless of skin tones or backgrounds. It will not matter as to how much he accomplishes or not, the "financial woes" were left to him by the previous president. Hopefully, the emphasis as in his campaign message was unity and with that as a focus Americans should all benefit from his presidency.

This author just could not imagine the many bigots from the past that are "turning over in their graves" as a result of America voting for a Black man. I wish it were possible to let them visit for a brief period of time to see into this century. God is good and He is good all of the time. White racists are looking forward to more members especially, especially, when our economy is going down. When the economy suffers the Klu Klux Klan tends to grow because many Whites did not vote for nor did they want a person of color to be president of these United States. When times get hard in America then some vicious and wanton Whites come looking for blood from people of color. Some people are "scared to death" because America now has a person of color running this country. There is only so much that a president can do, it takes the Congress and the Senate to help pass or deny bills and other legislature.

The Obama Family:

This new family in Washington, D.C., is the most popular family in America bar none. There are children once again in the White House. America will never again be the same; this is a "new millennium," one that has never been seen before.

Threats made to President Obama have been more numerous than to any prior president. The plot to kill him was uncovered by the police and the two main subjects have been arrested. This is a daily problem for the Secret Service they must be vigilant day and night to protect our Presidents' life. Christians united we must pray for our resident daily!

President Obama shattered the picture of a White male always being elected president however; there is still much work to be done in America. There has been tremendous progress over the years, but we have much to accomplish. Yet, we have much to be grateful for the progress made. Most Americans are still proud to stand up and say yes, I am an American. My prayers and hopefully the prayers of the entire nation will enable our new President to be outstanding and just and fair with all groups. He is a prime example of a multicultural person, and I thank God for that fact. Most Americans today are also multi -combinations of two or three groups. It should not be of any importance; the major concept is that we are all human!

Mrs. Michelle Obama is a lovely first lady, and so very elegant. When I saw her beside the Queen of England, I thought to myself she is also a queen! Then the two embraced, my tears began to roll, how I wish the world could embrace and solve all of our pressing problems. Your mother Mrs. Robinson it is so wonderful to have a grandma in the home for your two girls. They are truly blessed to have a mother and a father and also a grandmother in the home. As Americans we need to embrace our new President and what he is attempting to do for our country. America may not be aware of the prestige that is now growing for America in the world because of the new first family. Hopefully the American image will change in the world as a result of President Barack Obama!

Thanks to the many skilled and knowledgeable authors of today have a preponderance of materials to use now that all of the historical events of recent months have begun to expand and materials for writing are on the increase. Being grateful for all of the wonderful things that are going on in America today there is not much time left for ex-clusion these are the days for inclusion of **all Americans.**

This Legacy begins: With God the Father saying to Jesus Christ let us make man in our own image and likeness. God took a lump of dust from the earth and breathed into the nostrils the breath of life. Mankind was made into a living creature. God then made woman from a rib from Adams side. God saw that it was good. These two people populated the world at that time. Then came Noah and his family (descendants of Adam and Eve) the earth was filled with sin and wickedness continually, God was tired of it. This man Noah and his family, only did God save from the impending disaster that was to come upon the earth.

Noah and his family populated the earth and later Nimrod decided he didn't need God. He was going to find his way into heaven his way. He gathered workers and had them pile brick upon brick creating a tall tower. One day God noticed the tower and decided something had to be done to stop Nimrod. God and His son went down to earth and He changed the language and the brick maker did not understand the mortar, and the building stopped. After God changed the language he separated the land and divided it so that the group that understood each other bunched together and thus was the beginning of different speech and cultures.

Now the Legacy continues: With the African being the main theme and their efforts even when the land was connected they were explorers and traders with others. Their influence is known throughout the world, especially Mexico and some of the Caribbean Islands. Dr. Wiener found that the African artifacts were found also in northeastern section of America.

Africans were traveling, trading, and settling new lands and leaving their particular influence on the native people there. Often these groups mated and had offspring, continuing the cycle of human kind.

Some of the African travel included walking, going by raft, or boat. The replicas of their rafts are still found in some of the islands.

Thor Hyderdal duplicated the raft making techniques in 1969; he was very successful in taking his raft from western Africa to the Americas. This done to prove once and for all that Africans did traverse the Atlantic Ocean.

Africans made an indelible mark on Mexico as the heads of the gods are still in Mexico to this day. Mexicans made sacrifices to this god Ilixton. He had a large head with kinky-looking hair a broad nose and large lips. The characteristics were strictly African. (Please notice the front cover)

The Legacy continues: The civilization in Africa or nearby areas. Ancient Africans began to dominate their environment and to invent tools and methods of "iron smelting." The ventured far and wide across the Oceans and visited many places throughout the world. They even came as far as America according to Dr. Leo Wiener, Thor Hyderdal, Ivan Van Sertima, Lerone Bennett, and Dr. J. A. Rogers.

The Legacy continues: The sociological significance of race and ethnicity. This is important because sociologist do not believe that race is a major factor as it relates to the various groups throughout the world. However, they do concede the ethnicity is very valuable indeed. Ethnicity takes in languages, belief systems, clothing, food and the way of a people that distinguishes them from another group.

The Legacy continues: With the reintroduction of Africans to America; in the form of slavery. Africans had a form of slavery and so did most of the ancient world it was a way of life. However, the few African Chiefs had no idea of what the Europeans had in mind for their fellow Africans that were being sent for a payment of some kind. This was not the usual method that the Europeans used. Most Africans were caught in traps, and kidnapped when walking alone in the jungle. Traps were set and Africans were caught in them like you would capture an animal from the jungle. The majority of Africans were stolen very few were bought from Leaders. Slavery in Africa was very different from the slavery that was to be in America. When a tribe in Africa won a battle with an enemy tribe, the losers belonged to the winning tribe. The losing tribe could live and marry into the winning tribe, become a Leader.

There was nothing to stop the progress one could make within the winning tribal group. And of course, there was no problem with color as they were all the same or similar pigmentation

The slaves had to be very strong and determined to survive although slavery was made into a lifetime of bondage. God arranged in His time to free them. After all the Israelites were enslaved to the Egyptians for over 400 hundred years; this author's notes: God is no respecter of persons and if he enslaved His own people the Israelites than it seems feasible for Him to enslave Africans for the same reasons disobedience. In ancient times Portugal and Spain began to steal Africans from Africa back in the 1440's; slavery for the African Americans has a total of over 400 years. God in His own justification system saw to it that Israel was avenged, and thereby, it was necessary for Africans to suffer as the Israelites suffered under Black Egypt; had turned away from God as the Israelites had done.

The Legacy continues: African Americans/Blacks after slavery to the present. Involves the historical achievements and sacrifices they made to make America what it is today. Blacks were homeless and displaced and being told to live differently. Now they were to find a house and work and make money. This was new as the masters always provided a place to live and the work was automatic, without any pay! They had to struggle to get an education and to find employment.

The Legacy continues: African Americans had their faith in God and the Black Church. The Church has been an ever-present mainstay in the lives; of the African Americans during and after bondage. The people believed that God would make a way for them one day. And He did, God made it possible for President Abraham Lincoln to write the Emancipation Proclamation in 1862. The Congress and Senate pass this legal document that freed the slaves from bondage. Thank you Lord Jesus for the blessings and the privilege for being free at last!

Great strides have been made and more notable accomplishments have been provided to America from the African Americans.

For example, Washington, D.C. owes a great debt to the wonderful talents of **Dr. Benjamin Banneker**. When L'Enfant was disgruntled with the procedures and progress of the plaza he packed his blueprints and left. However, Banneker memorized the exact layout of the plaza, and he finished the work that L'Enfant had begun. For all of Banneker's diligence and perseverance there is a very short street with his name on it; but L'Enfant name is all over D.C., and the D.C., plaza is named for him. Somehow it seems that no matter how much an African American does- it is not "good enough."

Author's reflection: When I was a child my parents use to tell me that I had to be better than any student in my classes. I never understood the reason for this, but today I do understand, it should never have been this way but it was and still is in many instances even today.

In order to get promotions an African American has to be better by far. Remember the committee meeting of Texaco leaders, and the laughing joke about "the black jelly beans always being stuck at the bottom." That was not funny and I am glad they had to pay a large fine and promote the worthy candidates. That is only one small example of inadequate treatment that remains in many areas of America to this day. The obstacles and hurdles placed in the way have been "jumped over" and conquered one way or another. It is very difficult to keep good people down, and for the most part Blacks or African Americans are hard working, good parents and dedicated. Most Blacks or African Americans do not know their own history; therefore, whatever is said about the group is readily accepted. Most educational institutions have removed Black History from their curriculums. This author will give an example of a few of the inventors and their inventions.

Listed are just a few of the African American Inventors and their Inventions and/or discoveries that were made in America; from the past to present times:

Garrett Morgan- The three way stop light, in 1914 patented the gas mask. First chemical hair straightener, also established a newspaper called the Cleveland Call.

George Washington Carver- Produced over 300 products from the peanut. For example peanut butter and peanut products, which include stains and paints, printers, ink, axle grease, cooking oil. He also discovered many over 118 products from the sweet potatoes, products. Dr. Carver further discovered 75 products from the pecan that we are still using in America today. He also taught the planters about crop rotation.

Dr. Benjamin Banneker- He invented the almanac, the clock; he was a scientist and an inventor. He also completed the project for the Washington; D.C.'s L'Enfant plaza when the disgruntled L'Enfant packed up his blueprints and left.

Dr. Charles Drew-Doctor, researcher, inventor of blood plasma, which led to the blood banks, He was the first African American to get a Ph.D. from Columbia.

Dr. Shirley Jackson-modern day researcher invented the portable fax, touch tone phones, solar cell phones, and fiber optic cables to run cables underwater and around the world, the I.D. and call waiting while heading the Bell Laboratories.

Hopefully, Dr. Jackson is a relative of the Jackson family from Florida. (This author wanted to show that African Americans or Blacks are still making present day contributions)

Carter G. Woodson organized the first Negro history Week Celebration on the second week of February in 1926. The week celebration eventually became a moth long celebration, which is now known as Black History Month.

The term "**Buffalo Soldiers**" was a nickname given to African-Americans soldiers of the 10th regiment U.S. Army by the Native Americans they fought in 1866. Although several African-American regiments were created during the Civil War to fight alongside the Union Army, they were never given the respect that they deserved. Congress declared the first peacetime all Black regiment in the regular U.S. Army when it established the "Buffalo Soldiers."

Jesse Owens broke 4 world records in one afternoon at the Big Ten Championships on May 25, 1935; a year later, he upstaged Adolf Hitler by winning 4 gold medals (100m, 200m, 4x100m relay and long jump) at the 1936 Olympics in Berlin.

In 1900, **James Weldon Johnson** wrote with his brother the song "Lift Ev'ry Voice and Sing" on the occasion of Lincoln's birthday. The song became immensely popular in the Black community and became known as the "Negro National Anthem."

The African American Advisors to President Franklin D. Roosevelt were called the: Black Brain Trust."

Frederick Eversley, an African American sculptor, created a stainless steel sculpture of two wings –like shapes framed by neon lights at the entrance to the Miami International Airport.

In 1770, **Crispus Attucks**, whose father was African and mother was a Nantucket Indian, became the first casualty of the American Revolution when he was shot and killed in what became known as the Boston Massacre.

W.E.B. DuBois became the first African American to earn a Ph.D. from Harvard. He is perhaps best known for his work in founding the National Association for the Advancement of Colored people in 1909 and helping it to become the country's single most influential organization for African Americans.

Louis Latimer was the only African American engineer/scientist member of the elite Edison Pioneers research and development organization. Until Latimer's process for making carbon filaments, Edison's light bulbs would burn only a few minutes. Latimer's filament burned for hours.

Dr. Charles Drew was a leading researcher in the field of blood plasma preservation, an led a massive blood donation drive to provide the British with much- needed blood supplies during World War II.

Garrett Augustus Morgan invented a smoke hood in 196 that he used to rescue several men trapped by an explosion in tunnels under Lake Erie. The U.S. Army into the gas mask, which was used to protect soldiers from chlorine fumes during World War I, later refined this invention. He also invented an early version of a traffic signal that featured automated STOP and GO signs.

Matthew Henson, a Black explorer, accompanied Admiral Robert E. Peary on the first successful expedition to the North Pole in 1909. (It has been stated that it was he and not Peary that placed the U.S. flag at the North Pole, however, because he was second in line to Peary, he was not given the recognition that he deserved).

The son of escaped slaves from Kentucky; Elijah McCoy was born in Canada and educated in Scotland. Settling in Detroit, Michigan, he invented a type of lubricator for steam engines (patented 1872) and established his own manufacturing company. During his lifetime he acquired 57 patents.

Born the son of a French planter and a slave in New Orleans**, Norbert Rillieux** was educated in France. Returning to the U.S., he developed an evaporator for refining sugar, which he patented in 1846. Rillieux's evaporation technique is still used in the sugar industry and in the manufacture of soap and other products.

Benjamin O. Davis, Jr., became the first African American general in the U.S. Air Force in 1954.

Sir William Arthur Lewis, a professor economics at Princeton University, was the first African American to receive a Nobel Peace Prize. He received the award in 1979, which represents the highest level of accomplishment for an economist.

It seems that African Americans have made major contributions to America and to the world. Past and present inventors are still inventing and America is still the recipient. One would have to look far and wide; most of the time to see that the proper recognition has been forthcoming as it relates to Blacks or African Americans inventions or discoveries.

Dr. Ben Carson, the head Neurosurgeon at Johns Hopkins Hospital in Baltimore, Maryland. He was made ex famous in 1987 when he was flown to Ulm Germany to separate Siamese twins joined at the head. He is a Christian and was raised by a God- fearing mother. Her words of inspiration encouraged her two boys to be "as good as anyone else and to do better."

Again the Black church and faith has brought the group thus far, and with God's grace and guidance they will continue to be progressive and entrepreneurs into this new century. The church has been the stalwart for the black family it was a refuge during slavery, it was a haven after slavery, and it is a beacon for modern day families. This has been the main source where African Americans or Blacks were able to gain spiritual power, and strength to continue to strive.

Many Americans are of the belief that all is fine as far as race relations are concerned. The astute persons will realize that the problem remains. Yes, even President Obama is aware of the problems that still persist in America. There have been so many death threats on his life, but the secret service is attempting to keep that a private matter.

However, the racists, the bigots, and the skin-heads that hate are still doing damage to people of color in America. There should be none of this going on but it is. These type haters hide and wait for darkness to do their evil deeds.

There is a great racial divide still in America, with the vestiges of slavery and Jim Crow racism continues in one form or another. It would seem obvious that African Americans are citizens and cannot be controlled by hatred when there is so much love to be shared. Why would a strong independent nation like ours become subject to old patterns of division and hatred? This does not make any sense at all to a thinking, logical, and rational American.

Bigotry is not limited to the south anymore, now it is all across the nation. Cross burnings, and racist graffiti, threats, and intimidation is going on nationwide. These tactics did not work in past years and with Gods' help they will not succeed in this modern generation.

The Legacy continues: For some Blacks the "chains on the mind," syndrome is as real as the chains that were on the body during slavery. This means that there has to be a re-indoctrination concerning the wondrous historical contributions supplied by people from Africa. Perhaps the "playing field is not quite level" but it is not as far out of kilter as it was years ago. There is still hope and we must all pray and hope for a just and equal nation, which can only come about with the love of the Lord Jesus Christ and putting Him first in our lives, from the President to the lowly street cleaner. America, we can do this yes we can! We now have a sitting African American President this year 2010, America we can and we must eradicate this evil known as "racism."

Americans living in this land of the free and home of the brave, we all have much to be grateful for. There has been much progress toward "racial peace," but there is still lots left to do. Especially, there is a need for solidarity in the African American communities. They need to go back to a sense of community. It is not that integration is a "bad" thing; however, the sense of people hood/community no longer seems to exist. This book is dedicated to all of my Black, and White brothers and sisters in the Lord Jesus Christ. Especially, to the people of Greece, they were so honest and just that they wrote about many of the inventions and contributions made by Africans for the world's benefit. There should be a sense of added pride and a sense of thankfulness for the many contributions made by "our" forefathers from Africa to the world and to America. Blacks through the years have made tremendous Journey's that have impacted the world from looking back through history while continuing to move forward further into the Twenty First Century! May God richly bless each one of you and thanks for reading my book!

~FINIS~

REFERENCES

Chapter 1

The Origin of Humankind

[1] Genesis 2:7
[2] Ibid 2:10-15
[3] Ibid 11:1
[4] Ibid 11:6-9

Chapter 2

The Birth and Genealogy of Jesus: People of Color in the Bible:
Felder, Cain Hope (Editor) <u>The Original African Heritage Study Bible</u>

[1] Matthew 1:1-16
[2] Isaiah 53:1-12
3 Matthew 1:18
[4] Ibid 2:1-3
[5] P. 1377
[6] Daniel 7:9
[7] P. 4
[8] Revelation 1:14-15
[9] p. vii
[10] p. xv
[11] p. xii
[12] p. 3
[13] p. 1814 (a)
[14] p. 1814 (b)
[15] Peebles, James W. Preface page p. 1
[16] p. 4
[17] p. 334
[18] Deuteronomy 28:68
[19] Galatians 3:28
[20] 1 King 10:1
[21] Numbers 12:1
[22] Ibid 2:10
[23] Jeremiah 38:6
[24] Ibid 38:1-28
[25] Genesis 16:1
[26] 2 Kings 19:9-10
[27] Isaiah 37:9-10
[28] Genesis 41:45
[29] Mark 15:21
[30] Exodus 4:6-7

Chapter 3

Civilization in Africa

[1] Lerone Bennett Jr., <u>Before the Mayflower.</u> pg. 5 (a)
[2] Ibid. pg. 5 (b)
[3] Ibid. pg. 32
[4] Ibid. p. 5-6
[5] Bennett, Lerone Jr. p 24
[6] Rogers's pg 17
[7] Gerald Horne, Thinking and Rethinking U.S. History pg.19
[8] Carol Berkin et al, <u>American Voices</u>. p. 19
[9] Bennett p.5-6
[10] Ibid p. 6
[11] Rogers's p. 14
[12] Jackson, Man, God, and Civilization p. 284
[13] Van Sertima p. 17
[14] Rogers's p 16
[15] Rogers's p. 16
[16] Rogers's p. 18
[17] Bennett p.13
[18] Ibid p. 9-11
[19] Ibid p. 11
[20] Ibid p 46-47 Rogers's on Jackson
[21] Van Sertima p. 78
[22] Ibid p. 17
[23] Ibid p. 15-17
[24] Rogers's pg. 78
[25] Ibid p 59 (a)2
[26] Ibid p. 59(b)
[27] Van Sertima p. 256

Chapter 4

The Sociology of Race and Ethnicity

[1] Macionis, John J. p. 348
[2] Ibid p. 448
[3] Ibid p. 348
[4] Ibid p. 347
[5] Ibid p. 447

Chapter 5

Reintroduction of Blacks to Americas: The Black Family in Slavery

[1] Franklin, John Hope and Alfred A. Moss Junior., <u>From Slavery to Freedom.</u> P.32-33

[2] Horne, Gerald p. 55

[3] Ibid p. 61

[4] Rogers's p. 31 From Superman to Man

[5] Bennett, Lerone Jr. pg. 136

[6] Horne, Gerald p.59

[7] Jackson, John G. p. 306

[8] Franklin & Moss p. 106

[9] Bernard, Jesse Marriage and Family Among Negroes, p. 103-104

[10] Lynch, Willie, The Willie Lynch Law

[11] Van Sertima p.75

[12] Grimke-Drayton, William (reprint)w/permission 2007

[13] Rogers's p. 74 From Superman to Man

[14] Billingsley, Andrew, Dr. p. 61 Black Families in White America

[15] Franklin & Moss p. 103-104

Chapter 6

The Black Family from 1865—Present

[1] Billingsley, Andrew, <u>Black Families in White America</u>. Pg. 71
[2] Franklin, John Hope and Alfred A. Moss Junior, <u>From Slavery to Freedom</u>. Pg. 208
[3] Ibid. pg. 208
[4] Ibid p. 209
[5] Ibid p 215
[6] Ollin P. Moyd, <u>Redemption in Black Theology</u>. Pg. 201
[7] Macionis, John J. <u>Sociology</u>. Pg. 467

Chapter 7

The Original African Heritage Study Bible (Bible quotes and un-named pages)
The Black Church/Religion

[1] Psalm 68:21
[2] P. 1816
[3] Ibid 1816
[4] Ibid 1816
[5] Jackson, John G. p. 261
[6] Preface p. 1
[7] Rogers's p. 36
[8] Ibid p. 37
[9] Seaton p. viii
[10] Ibid p. viii
[11] Franklin & Moss p. 124-125
[12] Ibid p 94
[13] Franklin & Moss p. 125
[14] Cleage, Albert B. p. 5 Black Christian Nationalism New Direction for the Black Church
[15] Cone, James p. 79 Black Theology and Black Power
[16] Cleage, Albert B. p. 132
[17] Ibid p. 135-136
[18] Cone, James p 159
[19] Ibid p. 159
[20] Paris, Peter J. p.99 The Social Teaching of the Black Churches
[21] Ibid p. 100
[22] Browder, Anthony p. 3 From the Browder Files
[23] Ibid p 3
[24] Ibid p 3-4
[25] Welsing. Cress, Frances p. 170 The Isis Papers
[26] Ibid p 170
[27] Ibid p. 170
[28] Ibid p. 171

BIBLIOGRAPHY

Akbar, Na'im. <u>Chains and Images of Psychological Slavery</u>. Jersey City, NJ: New Mind Productions, 1991

Bennett, Lerone, Jr., <u>Before the Mayflower</u>: A History of the Negro in America (1619-1962) Johnson Publishing Co., Inc., Chicago, Ill Baltimore, MD.,1962.

Berkin, Carol, et. al. <u>American Voices</u>. Glenville, IL: Scott Foresman, 1992.

Bernard, Jessie. <u>Marriage and Family Among Negroes</u>. Englewood Cliffs, NJ: Prentice-Hall, Inc., 1966.

Billingsley, Andrew. <u>Black Families in White America</u>. Englewood Cliffs, NJ: Prentice-Hall, Inc., 1968.

Birnbaum, Norman, and Gertrude Lenzer. <u>Sociology and Religion, A Book of Reading</u>. Englewood Cliffs, NJ: Prentice-Hall, Inc., 1969.

"Black Church Celebrates Bicentennial." <u>Anchorage Daily News</u>, 7 Anchorage, Alaska, November 1992, 8(F).

Botkins, B.A. <u>Lay My Burdens Down</u>. Chicago, IL: University of Chicago Press, 1945.

Browder, Anthony T. <u>From the Browder File</u>. Washington, D.C.: The Institute of Karmic Guidance, 1989.

Brown, Richard D., and Stephen G. Rabe. <u>Slavery in American Society</u>. Lexington, MA: D.C. Heath and Co., 1976.

Carmichael, Stokely, and Charles V. Hamilton. <u>Black Power, The Politics of Liberation in America</u>. New York, NY: New York Vintage Books, 1967.

Cary, Lorene. <u>Black Ice</u>. New York, NY: Alfred A. Knopf, 1991.

Chapman, Abraham. Black Voices, an Anthology of Afro-American Literature. New York, NY: Times Mirror (Mentor Books from New American Library), 1968.

"Chromosome trail leads to African Adam." Anchorage Daily News, 26 May, 1995, 1(A). Anchorage, Alaska

Clark, Kenneth B. Dark Ghetto. New York, NY: Harper and Row, 1965.

Cleage, Albert B. Black Christian Nationalism New Directions for the Black Church. Detroit, MI: Luxor Publisher of the Pan-African Orthodox Christian Church, 1972.

Cone, James H. Black Theology and Black Power. New York, NY: Seabury Press, 1969.

Liberation: A Black Theology of Liberation. New York, NY: J.B. Lippincott Co., 1970.

For My People, Black Theology and the Black Church. Maryknoll, NY: Orbis Books, 1991.

God of the Oppressed. New York, NY: Seabury Press, 1975.

Cress-Welsing, Frances. The Isis Papers. Chicago, IL: Third World Press, 1991.

Davidson, Basil. The African Past. New York, NY: Grosset and Dunlap, 1964.

Drake, St Clair, and Horace Cayton. Black Metropolis, A Study of Negro Life in a Northern City. New York, NY: Harper and Row, 1945.

DuBois, W.E.B. The Negro American Family. Cambridge, MA: M.I.T. Press, 1909.

Elkins, Stanley M. Slavery, A Problem in American Institutional and Intellectual Life. New York, NY: Grosset and Dunlap, Inc., 1963.

Felder, Cain, editor. The Original African Heritage Study Bible (King James Version). Nashville, TN: James C. Winston Co., 1993.

Felder, Cain Hope. Stony the Road We Trod. Minneapolis, MN: Fortress Press, 1991.

<u>Troubling Biblical Waters. Race, Class and Family</u>. Maryknoll, NY: Orbis Books, 1992.

Franklin, John Hope and Alfred A. Moss, Jr. <u>From Slavery to Freedom</u>. 6th ed. New York, NY: McGraw Hill, Inc., 1988.

Frazier, E. Franklin. <u>The Black Bourgeoisie</u>. Glencoe, IL: The Free Press, 1957.

Black Bourgeoisie, The Rise of a New Middle Class in the United States. New York, NY: Collier Books (The Free Press), 1962.

<u>The Free Negro Family</u>. Nashville, TN: Fisk University Press, 1932.

<u>The Negro Church in America</u>. New York, NY: Schocken Books, 1974.

<u>The Negro Family in the United States</u>. Chicago, IL: University of Chicago Press, 1948.

Freund, Julien. <u>The Sociology of Max Weber</u>. New York, NY: Vintage Books Random House, 1969.

Grimke-Drayton, William (permission given to print December, 2007)

Harrison, Bob. <u>When God Was Black</u>. Concord, CA: Bob Harrison Ministries International, 1978.

Herskovits, Melville. <u>The Myth of the Negro Past</u>. Boston, MA: Beacon press, 1958.

Holly, Alonzo Potter. God and the Negro, Synopsis of God and the Negro of the Biblical Record of the Race of Ham. Nashville, TN: National Baptist Board, 1937.

Horne, Gerald. <u>Thinking and Rethinking US History</u>. New York, NY: The Council of Interracial Books for Children, Inc., 1988.

Hough, Joseph C., Jr. Black Power and White Protestants, A Christian Response to the New Negro Pluralism. New York, NY: Oxford University Press, 1968.

Jackson, John G. Introduction to African Civilization Citadel Press, Carol Publishing group, New York, New York, 1970

<u>Man, God and Civilization</u>. Secaucus, NJ: Citadel Press, 1972.

144

Jackson, Robert L. Church Building Through Evangelism. Columbus, GA: Brentwood Christian Press, 1989.

Johnson, James Weldon. God's Trombones, Seven Negro Sermons in Verse. New York, New York: Penguin Books, 1990.

Kardiner, Abram, and Lionel Ovesey. The Mark of Oppression. New York, NY: W.W. Norton Co., 1951.

Lincoln, C. Eric. The Black Church Since Frazier. New York, NY: Schocken Books, 1974.

The Negro Pilgrimage in America. New York, NY: Bantam Books, Pathfinder Editors, 1967.

Lynch, William, The Willie Lynch Letter: "The Making of a Slave," FCN Publishing Co., Reprinted, 2005

Macionis, John J. 7th ed. Prentice Hall, Englewood Cliffs, NJ: 1991.

Marx, Gary T. Protest and Prejudice, A Study of Belief in the Black Community. New York, NY: Harper Torch books (Harper and Row), 1969.

Moyd, Olin P. Redemption In Black Theology. Valley Forge, PA: 1979.

Paris, Peter J. The Social Teaching of the Black Church. Philadelphia, PA: Fortress Press, 1985.

Parsons, Talcott, and Kenneth B. Clark. The Negro American. Boston, MA: Beacon Press, 1966.

Pettigrew, Thomas F. A Profile of the Negro American. Princeton, NJ: D. Van Norstrand Co., 1964.

Pinkney, Alphonso. Black Americans. Englewood Cliffs, NJ: Prentice-Hall, 1969.

Quarles, Benjamin. The Negro in the Making of America. London: Collier Books (Division of Macmillan Publishing Co., Inc.), 1969.

Roberts, J. Deotis. Liberation and Reconciliation, A Black Theology. Philadelphia, PA: Westminster Press, 1971.

Rogers's, J.A. Africa's Gift to America, The Afro-American in the Making and Saving of the United States. New York, NY: Helga M. Rogers's, 1961.

<u>Sex and Race</u>, Volumes I through III. New York, NY: Helga M. Rogers's, 1944.

<u>World's Greatest Men of Color</u>, Volumes I and II. New York, NY: Collier Books, 1964.

"Pope Begs Forgiveness for Slave Trade." <u>Oakland Tribune</u>, 7 March, 1992.

Smith, Wallace Charles. <u>The Church in the Life of the Black Family</u>. Valley Forge, PA: Judson Press, 1985.

Stallings, James O. <u>Telling the Story, Evangelism in Black Churches</u>. Valley Forge, PA.: Judson Press, 1988.

Stampp, Kenneth M. <u>The Peculiar Institution, Slavery in the Ante-Bellum South</u>. New York, NY: Vintage Books (Division of Random House), 1956.

Staples, Robert. <u>The Black Family, Essays and Studies</u>. Belmont, CA: Wadsworth Publishing Co., 1991.

Stewart, Warren H., Sr. Interpreting <u>God's Word in Black Preaching</u>. Valley Forge, PA: Judson Press, 1984.

<u>The Holy Bible</u> (King James Version). Camden, NJ: Thomas Nelson, Inc., 1970. Van Sertima, Ivan. <u>They Came Before Columbus</u>. New York, NY: Random House, 1976.

Washington, Booker T. <u>Up From Slavery</u>. New York, NY: Doubleday and Company (Bantam Books), 1959.

Washington, Joseph J. Black Religion, The Negro and Christianity in the United States. Boston, MA: Beacon press, 1964.

Washington, Preston Robert. <u>God's Transforming Spirit, Black Church Renewal</u>. Valley Forge, PA: Jedson Press, 1988.

Weber, Max. <u>The Sociology of Religion</u>. Boston, MA: Beacon Press, 1956.

<u>Webster's Collegiate Dictionary</u>, Tenth Edition, Springfield, MA: Merriam-Webster, Inc., 1988.

Wegener, Alfred. <u>The Origin of Continents and Oceans</u>. New York: Dover Press. 1966

Wiener, Leo. <u>Africa and The Discovery of America</u>. Brooklyn, NY: A&B Book Company, 1992, reprinted.

Williams, Chancellor. <u>The Destruction of Black Civilization</u>. Chicago, IL: Third World Press, 1974.

Notes on the Author

Laura Lee King attended U.C. Berkeley in the 1960's and is a graduate from the International Seminary with a Ph.D. Laura writes children stories also. She is retired and works for herself providing services for others. Laura is an Evangelist and is dedicated to working for God. Her faith is very deep and she knows that she can do nothing without the Lord Jesus in her life. Laura is a mother and grandmother.

This book <u>The Legacy: Looking Back While Moving Forward</u> has been in process for many years, it is a joy to finally have it completed. All thanks and praises to Jesus Christ my life! It is hoped that you the reader will find the true reason for this book to have been written.

Made in the USA
Charleston, SC
17 June 2010